the
gentile

Dedicated to Kathleen Touchstone

Also by D. S. Lliteras:

The Thieves of Golgotha

In a Warrior's Romance

The Llewellen Trilogy:

In the Heart of Things

Into the Ashes

Half Hidden by Twilight

JUDAS
THE
GENTILE

A NOVEL

D.S. LLITERAS

HAMPTON ROADS
PUBLISHING COMPANY, INC.

Cover design by Marjoram Productions
Cover art by Chet Jezierski

For information write:

Hampton Roads Publishing Company, Inc.
134 Burgess Lane
Charlottesville, VA 22902

Or call: (804)296-2772
FAX: (804)296-5096

e-mail: hrpc@hrpub.com
Web site: http://www.hrpub.com

If you are unable to order this book from your local
bookseller, you may order directly from the publisher.
Quantity discounts for organizations are available.
Call 1-800-766-8009, toll-free.

Library of Congress Catalog Card Number 99-71617

ISBN 1-57174-144-5

10 9 8 7 6 5 4 3 2 1

Printed on acid-free paper in the United States

Contents

Night (New Testament)

First Watch—6 to 9 p.m.
Second Watch—9 to 12 a.m.
Third Watch—12 to 3 a.m.
Fourth Watch—3 to 6 a.m.

A new day starts at sunset.

Hear, O Israel,
The Lord is our God,
The Lord is One.

—DEUTERONOMY 6:4

What is truth?

—JOHN 18:38

Iesus Nazarenus Rex Iudaeorum

Do I contradict myself?
Very well then I contradict myself,
(I am large, I contain multitudes.)

—WALT WHITMAN

Time is space and not chronological.

CHAPTER 1
Before Sunset

"My mouth is a deadly weapon. It's full of venom and deceit and now . . . now, remorse. My mouth is a deadly weapon." Judas plunked his face downward toward his cradled arms and tipped over a cup full of wine with one of his elbows as his parallel forearms slid along the top of the table to cushion his forehead. The liquid spread its crimson influence across the rough wooden surface and back-washed against the sleeves of his tunic. He did not bother to lift his head when he felt its wetness reach the skin of his forearms.

Dinah, the matron barmaid and owner of this Roman-fashioned tavern that was situated just outside the northern city gate and along the road leading toward Golgotha, began sopping up the spilled wine with a rag.

"At least you're not enjoying the ghoulish spectacle of their suffering." She looked at the two tightly knotted groups of men that were congregating near the single large window facing the distant hill. "Look at them: the pigs. I had hoped I wouldn't have to bear my clients' enjoyment over their death, but my only trustworthy girl is having a baby right now."

Judas lifted his head and finally acknowledged her. "You speak as if you have more than a disinterest in his execution."

"Theirs, you mean. There are three of them. My man is one of them."

"I didn't understand what the hell he was talking about most of the time." The distance in Judas's eyes finally infected the tone of his voice. "He was everybody's man."

"Who? Azriel? Fat chance."

Judas sat up on his stool and reached for more composure. "No. Jesus. Was your Azriel a bandit?"

"Aren't we all in the eyes of Rome?"

"Yes. I suppose." Judas untied his purse from his leather belt and dropped it on the table. "More wine. And plenty of it. I never want to see my cup empty."

"If that's all—"

"Silver. All of it—what's left of it."

"Then I'll be sure to pour the wine myself."

"Good. Pour for both of us."

Dinah sought out her assistant, Lila, to instruct her to take over the long serving bench and secured two cups and a large pitcher from behind the long bench. Then she positioned the empty pitcher under one of the wine skins and began filling it.

Dinah's long and fitted tunic did not disguise her plump and buxom figure. And aside from a bit of embroidery running along the edge of her collar and a blue linen girdle wrapped around her waist, her outer garment was plain down to her bare feet.

With age threatening to dull the remaining edge of her fading beauty, she relied on her forthright character and friendly personality to heighten the surviving qualities of her attractiveness. However, even without these compensations, she was a handsome looking woman with steady eyes and moist lips, with balanced features and a rich complexion. Her long braided hair was thick and brown, clean and perfumed and bareheaded—unless she had to go to the market or into Jerusalem to conduct other business; until then, her upper mantle, a simple wrap to cover her head and upper body when she stepped outside, hung on one of the wine skin pegs behind the long bench.

As soon as the pitcher was full, she joined Judas at his table, set the cups down, and poured wine into both of them. Then she sat down on the stool adjacent to his.

Judas peered at her after drinking half his cup. "You have a strange way of mourning for your man."

"It's no stranger than your own sorrow. Was he a relative?" She noted his surprise.

"In a manner of speaking, yes. Yes. He was my . . . my—" He brought the cup of wine to his mouth and drank it to the bottom.

She refilled the cup as soon as he set it down on the table and did not press him for the rest of his answer. They both remained silent for a long while.

Judas wore a long-sleeved seamless tunic made of light wool. Its full length was cut fairly straight and extended to his ankles where there were slits on each side of the hem to allow for increased mobility. A leather belt around his waist kept the billowing garment close to his body and provided a means to secure his leather purse. Sandals protected his feet and a tightly woven cap made of wool and worn without a cloth wrap protected his head—although it exposed his long hair. From head to toe, he was dressed without color or sparkle and, therefore, the natural beige of ordinary wool, the browns of rough leather, and the complete lack of jewelry gave the general impression that he was a man without distinction.

Judas facial features were strong, particularly his hawk-like nose and large dark eyes that constantly darted from side to side with worry. His beard and mustache were short and well-groomed as was the black wavy hair on his head. He appeared to be an ordinary man—neither wealthy nor poor and, yet, neither a craftsman nor a scholar. These were a blend of contradictions that caused immediate suspicion in the minds of those who had any kind of interaction with him.

Judas reached for his cup, but he did not lift it off the table. "I was destined to do what I did."

"If . . . if you say so," Dinah said, trying to figure out what he meant.

"I had to . . . to discredit him. It's a very low form of betrayal."

"Had to? Who?"

The edges of his mouth curled downward into a grotesque crescent that intensified his scowl. "Only the Romans listened."

"The Romans don't care about anything that isn't political," Dinah said flatly.

"They also care about money."

"That's right. They execute thieves and murderers and those who don't pay their taxes."

"You don't believe me."

"Believe what?"

Judas stood up and gawked in the direction of the open window. He pointed toward Golgotha. "That man wanted to bear the cross."

"I believe there must be something in this wine."

"Don't humor me, woman."

"I told you, one of those men is mine." She stood up and leveled her defiant eyes at Judas. "And I don't need what's left of your silver."

He averted his eyes from hers and sat back down. "All I'm saying—" He looked up into her eyes displaying the full darkness of his torment. "I . . . I was necessary. What I did was . . . was wanted of me." A tear rolled down his left cheek. "I'm to receive no credit—whatever that is. How am I to bear this?"

"Who knows. But from whatever direction it's viewed, it seems you're an informer."

"Don't judge me."

Dinah sat back down with him. "Who the hell am I to judge?" She indicated the tight throngs of men enjoying the spectacle from her tavern's window. "But you can be sure that once they leave here, they'll turn their discriminating backs to us and, if forced to look around in acknowledgment, they will cast long accusing shadows as they look down at the likes of us."

"Us?" he said with resentment.

She quickly transformed her contempt into amusement. "You hypocrite."

He lowered his head in shame. "I'm sorry."

"That you are. But I understand. It's hard breaking a lifelong habit."

"But . . . but the likes of us?"

"Yes. The dark side. We are necessary, you know. Where else does the light come from?"

He looked toward the window. "From . . . from God?"

"Good heavens." She made no attempt to hide her disgust. "You religious types are all the same. My man Azriel was right: we all live like stupid rats and die like hungry dogs." She rose from Judas's table. "I need to look after my customers."

"I'm not going anywhere." He drank deeply from his cup, then spoke carelessly. "I've a whole purse of silver to drink up."

She quickly bent toward him and spoke through clenched teeth. "Quiet, now." Then she whispered vehemently at him. "Talk like that will only draw more attention to yourself and cause us trouble."

"Alright, alright." His irritability inspired him to raise his cup to his mouth, gulp down what was left of the wine, then lower his head as he set the empty cup back on the table.

Dinah caught Lila's attention and directed her to continue refilling Judas's cup while she saw to the comfort of her other clients—particularly those standing at the window.

Another man entered the tavern and scanned the small crowd until he recognized Judas. He was a thin, scraggly bearded, mean-looking sort with a ragged length of cloth wound around his shaggy head and tied in the back. He wore a tattered pair of sandals and a filthy sackcloth tunic woven from coarse fiber and gathered at the waist by several wraps of leather. He shifted his weight onto one leg as he waited until Lila filled Judas's cup, then approached him.

Dathan stood before Judas in silence, studying his somber behavior. He startled Judas with his abruptness. "Why do you brood so much over this man, Jesus? I hear his trial before the procurator was nothing—one of many just alike."

"From Pilate's viewpoint, I'm sure," Judas flared, recognizing Dathan's voice. "Unimportant."

"And yours?"

Judas finally lifted his head from its stooped position at the table and focused his watery eyes on Dathan. "My view? I don't know."

"For heaven's sake, look at you. You're spoiling your cup of wine with tears."

"I can't help myself."

"Convert."

Judas clenched the edge of the table with both hands to display his resentment. "What?"

"You're all the same."

"He should not be hanging on the wood!"

"Calm yourself, Judas. Rome has seen to that. Not you nor I. You are free of his blood before the eyes of God."

"What kind of God allows an innocent man to die?"

"Ahh, you have it now, convert. It's the crux of our religion." Dathan snatched Judas's cup of wine and took a deep drink. A broad grin dressed his countenance after he lowered the cup from his lips and set it back on the table near Judas. "You wanted a silent and invisible God, so now you have him."

"Then . . . then what's the point?"

Dathan looked around to be sure he couldn't be heard. "What's the point of any God? Look around you: Palestine has been filled with Gods. What good have any of them been?"

"You speak like a pagan."

"I have my doubts. But no matter: I was born a Jew—belief doesn't matter. But you . . . you are—"

"Were—"

"Alright. Were a gentile. And your belief is everything to you. Without it you are nothing."

"And I take that seriously."

"That's my point exactly, convert."

"Quit calling me that."

Dathan assaulted Judas with a grin. "See?"

"What?"

"You lack humor."

"What does that have to do with my demand?"

"Think about it. We believe in a God who does not appear. Other peoples have had the sense to reject him. But not the people of Israel. Nooo. We chose him. Don't you see the absurd humor in that?"

"No."

"No! We are clowns. And the Greeks, the Romans, the world laughs at us. We . . . we laugh at ourselves even. Especially."

"Why? If our God is nothing."

"Because . . . because nothing is all we have."

"You make too little sense to me, Dathan."

"I don't deny that. And the longer you believe, the closer you'll come toward understanding this denial."

"Perhaps." Judas picked up his cup and finished what was left of the wine. "But none of this is helping me to understand why that rabbi is dying from crucifixion at this moment."

Dathan noticed that Judas placed his hand over the empty cup to indicate that no wine was to be poured. He rose from the table. "He was condemned before he was arrested. Besides, I hear he condemned himself with his own words. There's not much you can do for a man like that."

"I've heard the same. Words. They were simply words."

"When you proclaim yourself a king or a prophet or perhaps . . . perhaps even a messiah, you have everybody with power as your enemy."

"He spoke of love and peace and brotherhood."

Dathan shrugged his shoulders after taking his thirsty eyes from Judas's cup. "All I can say is Pilate heard revolution from his lips, Herod feared insurrection, and our high priest's clan ignored his type of lunacy. Nobody wanted him around."

"Except the people."

"The people! Judas, you are quite stupid. Beggars and lepers and whores followed him. Not people who toiled on the land or worked on the sea."

"They used to be people. Rome and Herod have made them what they are."

"They! They?" Dathan audibly inhaled, then exhaled. "Well, *they* are now unclean and degraded—and expendable. *They* have no place for consideration. Not even by those of us with the courage to have become bandits—poor bastards: most of us will die just like that man, Jesus."

"My Master."

"Whoa. You've taken him too seriously, Judas."

"You weren't with him."

"And I'm glad. Because with my luck, there would have been a fourth man dying at Golgotha today—*me*. Yeah, that's my luck. And what about those other two who are suffering alongside your ... *your master*? Why not cry for them as well? They're no more or less nothing than he."

"I don't know their ... I've never met them."

"Then you're shallow and don't deserve the comfort of my continued company."

"You don't fool me, Dathan. You've engaged me in this conversation for the wine and nothing more."

"Maybe. And why not take advantage of a fool?"

Judas stood up in a display of anger. "I've had enough of you for one sitting."

"And I've enough of you for one lifetime." Dathan stood his ground, remaining face to face with Judas. "You're a joke among us, Judas. The word is out on you. Ganto wants to—" He nervously licked his lips. "He wants nothing more to do with you. You were supposed to kill him, not betray him—Ganto's furious. The word's been passed." He became paranoid. "You're in grave danger. My telling you this is a gift. Leave Palestine. At least, Jerusalem. Go back to Greece or . . . or wherever it is you come from."

"I will not."

Dathan pressed his face closer to Judas's. "You've helped to make a martyr of him."

"That's not so."

"We needed a warrior messiah, Judas. But all we have now is another spiritual messiah diluting Israel's armed rebellion against Rome."

"I kissed him."

"You disobeyed Ganto's orders."

"The arrest caught me off guard."

Dathan backed away toward the door leading out of the tavern. "If things got out of hand, you were supposed to kill him, convert."

Judas threw the empty cup at him. It smashed against the wall and caused a momentary commotion among the other clients in the tavern. "Get out before I put my hands on you!"

The two throngs of men at the window disassembled like an agitated swarm of bees and diverted their attention toward Judas's table.

Dinah rushed over to Dathan. "Go on. Do as he says. Get out."

"Having any trouble, Dinah?" one of the men asked.

"No, no. No trouble," she said.

Dathan pointed an icy finger at Judas. "Don't worry. I'll not inform Ganto of your whereabouts. But somebody will. You're destined for a bad end." He assaulted Judas with a cruel broken smile. "Thanks for the wine, you fool." He dashed out of the tavern anticipating Judas's increased anger.

Judas began to go after Dathan, but Dinah stepped in front of him. "Out of my way, woman."

"Not a lover's quarrel, is it Dinah?" one of the men shouted. The others laughed.

Dinah gestured with a terse sweep of the hand for the lot of them to stay out of this affair while she maintained most of her focus on Judas. "There'll be others waiting for you out there, believe me. His kind never works alone."

"I'm his kind," Judas said.

"No you're not. Please. Be wise. Have another cup of wine. On the house." Dinah surveyed her other customers and took advantage of their growing amusement. "In fact, I offer a cup of wine on the house for everybody."

This delighted her customers, especially the two groups of men standing near the large window. They resumed their drinking and speculative chatter concerning the dying men on the hill, while everybody else returned to their tables and their wine.

After Dinah was certain that Lila was preparing the necessary pitchers to pour everybody more wine, she placed a gentle hand on Judas's shoulder. "Please, let's not have anymore trouble." She waited in silence until Judas went back to his table. "I'll bring you a clean cup."

Judas sat down and slowly stretched his arms before him with the palms of both hands gliding along the surface of the table. He remained silent until his arms were fully extended and framing his purse of silver. "They wouldn't take this money."

Dinah motioned Lila to bring her another cup as she joined Judas at his table again. "You fool. The deed was done."

"No, no. You don't understand. Caiaphas' priestly clan would have nothing to do with it—with me!"

"Incidental," said Dinah.

Lila placed an empty cup in front of Judas, exchanged the serving pitcher already on the table with a fresh one, and left Dinah to tend to her special client.

"That's right," Judas said bitterly. "This purse is incidental. Even the five pieces I gave to the centurion was unnecessary."

"I don't understand you. This veneer is wasted on me."

"Woman, this is not about greed," Judas said irritably. "Nor was my motive a quest for power."

"What else is there?"

"Liberation."

"A nice word for treachery and betrayal."

"Treachery, perhaps—he is innocent. But betrayal—the grinding wheel of Rome's authority was already in motion. It's always in motion. There was nothing anybody could have done for him. His destruction was assured." Judas hiccuped. "Betrayal? My attempt added nothing."

Dinah finally poured wine into his cup from the pitcher at their table. "Well, you certainly didn't try to help."

"I wasn't supposed to. We were on the same side. Truly. Only—our ideas, my allegiance, our methods for accomplishing—"

"This liberation?"

"Yes—were different." He drank his wine to the bottom, set the cup down hard, and looked straight into Dinah's eyes. "He wanted liberation in another world and I wanted it in . . . in—where's this kingdom in heaven?"

Her silence lasted for several moments. "Well. It seems you've both lost your place—and your battle."

"Yes." Judas blinked his haunted eyes to gain better focus. "And according to any sensible person, this would be clear." He looked toward the window in the direction of Golgotha. "But what is sensible?" Judas trembled.

"He was a clever man. He should have been able to get away!"

"So—you really knew this man, Jesus, who's being crucified with my man."

"We traveled together, yes … yes, I told you."

"And Azriel, my man—did you ever?—"

"No, no." Judas fluttered his hands impatiently at her while keeping both elbows planted on top of the table. "Sorry. Never met the man. If he'd been lucky, his name would have been—"

"If he'd been lucky, he'd be sitting on your stool right now."

Judas was darkly amused by this woman. "Good one. The poor bastards. All of us. Such … poor … bastards. We are condemned."

"Your remorse has an odd ring."

"My plans failed. We are politically dead. The poor shall continue to starve."

"I could have told you that. I could have saved you from your present suffering."

"You know nothing."

"I'm taxed!" She snatched the pitcher off the table and carelessly poured more wine into his cup.

"Still … you know nothing."

Judas picked up his refilled cup of wine and drank so deeply and guzzled so quickly that wine trickled past both sides of his mouth, staining the front of his tunic. He lowered the cup to the table, after it was completely drained, and recklessly pushed it away with the back of his forearm.

If Dinah hadn't reached for the cup, it would have fallen and shattered on the hard mud floor.

"I've no wish to pick up broken clay all night on account of you."

"More wine."

Dinah remained motionless with the empty cup in her hand. "Not if you continue in this manner."

"Then leave me be." Judas lowered his head onto the table as if it were too heavy for him and crossed his arms above his crown to cover the sides of his face.

Dinah set the cup on the table, stood up, and went to the window where a number of her clients were still watching the three crucified men. There was not much to see from this distance, but the combination of wine and speculation kept them interested in the static scene.

"You've a live one at that table, Dinah," one of the men confided.

"I've seen you in that condition before, Gilgal."

A couple of his friend's laughed. Gilgal shoved away the nearest one with masculine affection. He winked at Dinah. "But I don't ever remember receiving so much attention from you."

"That's because you were too drunk to notice, you idiot."

This time both groups of men laughed.

"You tell him, Dinah," said the largest man in both groups. "He's never done a very good job of holding his wine."

Gilgal grabbed his groin with his left hand. "And you can hold this if you want to."

"That's right," Dinah said. "It only takes one hand to cover that one up."

Gilgal's face turned red as he felt the playful humiliation behind the explosive laughter of his comrades. "I've never heard you complain."

"It's my business not to." She noticed that Gilgal was beginning to frown in earnest. "Oh, go on. Don't take me seriously." She kissed Gilgal on the cheek.

"There you go, Gilgal," the largest man among them said. "A free kiss from Dinah is a rare thing."

"Let's drink to Gilgal's good fortune," one of the other men said.

Dinah kissed Gilgal's other cheek. "Lila, fill their cups again to the brim."

And as Lila recharged their cups, Dinah collected several denarii and a few coppers that paid for earlier cups. During the entire time, however, Dinah was fully aware of Azriel's remote presence. She snatched several glances out the window. But Azriel was at such a great distance from her window that she couldn't tell which one of the three figures on the wood was him. It took everything she had in her to hold back her tears and to project a lively spirit among her patrons. She managed to fool all but two of her customers, who were seated at the most private table in the establishment, near a dark corner where they were partially concealed behind the opposite end of the long serving bench. They were a serious looking pair and, by the look of them, were neither peasant farmers nor craftsmen.

To obscure their faces from Judas, both Reuben and Simeon had left their upper mantles draped over their heads and their lower mantles thrown across their shoulders. In most indoor establishments, the choice of not shedding either or both mantles while engaged indoors by the hour would have drawn a number of suspicious glances. But not in Dinah's tavern, where cautious behavior was a habit by those who were constantly—even recently—on the run from imperial forces. Like so many, they remained ready to go at a moment's notice, remained always alert. They knew that a single word of warning from Dinah, or from one of her assistants, was not to be questioned—they knew Dinah's reliable alarm was only a single step ahead of a raid from Herod's police or from a Roman detachment or from militia of any kind.

The darkest of the two surreptitiously glanced in Judas's direction. "Poor Dinah."

"Poor Azriel, you mean. He's the one who's dying on Golgotha."

"Yeah. But look where she's at—and with whom."

"That Judas is beginning to unravel—he's becoming dangerous, Simeon. The son of a bitch is more ambitious than he lets on."

"Aren't we all?"

"He has political ambitions."

"The poor wretch hasn't the temperament, Reuben."

"Then somebody needs to tell him."

"It's too late. He's betrayed Ganto."

"Well, I couldn't have assassinated Jesus."

"And now he openly spends Ganto's silver—bribe money that should have been returned." Reuben shook his head. "He's crazy. And that makes him dangerous. The leader of that prophet's band has gotten him all twisted inside. Just look at him more closely."

"He seems possessed," said Simeon.

"You can bet every silver piece you can lay your hands on that demon spirits are at work." Reuben indicated the window with a slight thrust of his jaw. "That Jesus was a shrewd manipulator. He knew which ropes to pull. I've heard that nobody could match either his wit or his talent for argument."

"Neither of which helped him against Rome," Simeon stated coldly.

"But we're not talking about Pilate, we're talking about that idiot over there. You'd have thought Judas could have seen he was outmatched. No, worse—not an able leader."

"Still—don't underestimate him. Why do you think he chose the common name of Judas to go by?"

"Bah! He's still a convert. That Corinthian whatever-his-true-name-is will never blend in among us. He'll always be a gentile's pawn."

"Still—he's a shrewd worm."

"Yeah. But like all of his kind, they're only good at getting into positions of control. Yet, once there, they don't know what the hell to do. It's as if getting there and being there are two separate processes."

"I wouldn't know anything about that. Royal pretenders and politicians are the same to me." Simeon lowered his head toward his cup to take a furtive drink of his wine. "Most of those kind are corrupt, as well."

"Would-be prophets and their henchmen. Crap! They make me sick with their accumulation of favors and the misuse of their follower's donations."

Simeon stole a glance in Judas's direction. "As if they can afford it."

"We, my friend. We." Reuben shook his head in disgust. "The burden of taxes drove us off our land and put us in the desperate circumstances that we are presently in—on the run from Rome and Herod."

"And our priests. Don't forget our greedy clan of priests."

"Yeah, yeah." Reuben drank some of his wine, then lowered his cup with a sudden need for justification. "We didn't choose thievery as a way of life." He began to smolder with anger. "The greedy bastards."

"Easy, Reuben. You're beginning to draw attention to us."

"I don't care about them or about revolution." His anger turned into disdain. "Freedom. What a joke. All I want is to set right the things I was wronged."

Simeon stared bitterly into his cup as he stirred its contents by moving it in a tight circular pattern over the surface of the table. "Nothing will bring back our families."

"My children starved and ... and—"

"So did my wife and . . . and —"

Neither one of them could finish the memories of their losses. They sat there for a while, brooding over their wine until the sound of Simeon's cup scraping along the table's surface began to irritate Reuben.

"Stop that, damn it." Then Reuben continued the thread of their former discussion in an effort to compensate for the effects of his latter outburst. "Like I said, these aspiring prophets—"

"Messiahs—"

"Whatever—make me sick. Especially when they take food out of the mouths of their following."

"True, true. These manipulators are simply men with the courage to speak—it seems."

"With the audacity to speak, you mean."

"The what?"

"The balls."

"Ah. Right."

"Anyway, that Judas needs to make up his mind where his allegiance lies."

"To himself, I think."

"I'm beginning to believe you're right." Reuben stared openly at the unconscious Judas. "You know, if he were really smart, he would have allied himself with a more practical leader."

"But I heard his brigand chief, Ganto, urged him to become one of Jesus' followers."

"True. But it became obvious even to me that there was little fruit to gain from that Jesus band. How many of them do you think were enlisted into Ganto's band by Judas's association with Jesus?"

"Probably none."

"Exactly. Judas should have cut and run by now and, yet—there, look: even you can see that he remains tied to that bunch. Why?"

Simeon shrugged his shoulders. "I'll not have anything more to do with him."

"Me neither. Especially since Rome has severed the head from that bunch. If they don't remain underground, Pilate is liable to hack up the rest of them in their frightened confusion."

"You mean, with the aid of Herod's secret police, crucify the lot of them."

"Damn right, Simeon. Say, you're not so ignorant as you often sound."

Uneasily. "Well don't give me too much credit."

"When have I ever done that?" Reuben gulped down a large portion of his wine. He lowered his cup feeling quite satisfied. "But when you're right, you're right. What's another set of mass crucifixions among many? And if you and I can see that this leftover group of Jesus' has the potential for making more trouble among the people, surely both Pilate and Herod have taken notice."

"I'm surprised the lot of them haven't been seized already. Especially since there are many in Jerusalem who are beginning to consider him the Messiah."

"And just as many, a king," Reuben added.

"That takes care of both Rome and Herod with one stroke. The damn Edomite."

Reuben was startled. "You mean, Herod."

"Of course. Foreigners. Both of them."

Reuben pondered over Simeon's obvious statement. "Foreigners. Very, very true." He finished his wine. "In fact, we need to get the word out among the others."

"About Jesus?"

"That goes without saying." Reuben leaned closer to Simeon. "As you've forewarned, our concern is more with Judas, remember? We shouldn't have anymore to do with him. He knows us and how we operate. If he should be arrested for his continued association with those followers of Jesus' and tortured—well, you can imagine the rest."

"I already have." Simeon shuddered. "Crucifixion is not to my liking." He finished his wine.

"Nor mine."

"I don't even like witnessing Rome's public display of this punishment."

"That's to your credit, my friend. Speaking of the devil. Look. Judas seems to be stirring."

"By God, you're right. Whoa, look at him. He's in an awful state."

"We better get out of here before he finally recognizes one of us," Reuben said. "There's no time like the present to begin breaking all ties with him. Wait for me outside while I pay for our wine."

"Right."

They both rose from their table and separated. Simeon was careful not to draw attention to himself as he left, while Reuben motioned Dinah toward him.

He placed a coin in her hand. "Use the rest of this to pay for that man's wine."

"I believe he's plenty of his own money," she said. "Don't I know you?"

"Then make sure he continues to drink more than his share of wine."

Dinah studied Reuben with open suspicion. "What queer motive is this?"

"He's a friend."

"Then you must understand what lies below his apparent dark mood."

"No. We all have our troubles."

"Then why not sit with him and help?" Dinah noticed that she struck an open wound. "And the other, the one who was just with you—was he not his friend?"

"That's right."

"Then stay."

"I can't, woman." The tone in his voice became firm. "And that's enough of this, you hear?"

Dinah closed her hand into a fist as if she were concealing the coin. "Sorry. I don't wish to meddle into affairs that are not my own."

"That's a wise course of action." He backed away from her in response to a sudden sense of urgency and stumbled over a stool. This caught Judas's attention; he recognized Reuben immediately.

"Reuben, my friend! I've been looking all over for you and the others."

"You . . . you have? What others?"

"Come here and sit down." Judas fixed his blurry eyes on him. "Share a cup of wine with me."

Reuben was trapped and he knew it. He looked at Dinah with disdain as he threw a whisper at her. "We'll talk again, later."

Dinah concealed her fear because she was not about to be intimidated in her own establishment. "Not if I decide otherwise," she murmured. "Sit down. I'll bring another cup to you."

Reuben turned from her and approached Judas as if he had leprosy. He reluctantly sat down at his table. "What are you doing with yourself these days?"

"I'm drowning my sorrows with wine, isn't that obvious?"

"Over . . . over what?"

"Over another crucifixion."

Reuben turned toward the window as if he sought further clarification from the direction in which Judas gazed. "Oh, that. Bah! He was just another charismatic leader—a magician."

"No, no. This one was different."

"Bullshit. They all view themselves—no—proclaim themselves as the new King of the Jews."

"This Jesus was different, I tell you."

"Look at yourself, Judas. Who are you trying to convince? He's a tortured peasant like the rest of us—he's nothing."

"But he spent so much time proclaiming—no—verifying his ancestral lineage to the House of David."

"Anybody can present seals and carry scrolls. Shit. Genealogy is for the rich."

"No, no—"

"Alright, read them—so what. Few of us read. And that means few of us can verify that which can be read."

"He performed—"

"Ha, better yet!"

"He performed miracles."

"I've heard. A wonder worker. A magician, I told you. Crap! Isn't there anything these damn royal pretenders wouldn't do to gain a following?"

"That's just it," Judas said. "He didn't care about having a following."

"Then why did he speak among the people?"

"To share."

"What?"

"His . . . his love."

"Right: nothing. What a clever character. This bandit made a complete profit."

"He took nothing."

"He ate their food and slept under their roofs, didn't he?"

Judas reached for his cup and discovered it was empty. "Yes."

Reuben continued to bait him now that he was confident in handling Judas. "Drank their wine. Flirted with their women."

"Nothing's wrong with any of that."

"Careful, Judas. You've fallen under this man's spell."

"I've not."

Reuben smiled at him. "Well—good. Because this supposed anointed one is—well, as you can see for yourself—is not likely to bring deliverance to our people. The fool spoke too much of peace and . . . and—"

"Love."

Reuben spat on the ground and actually threw a hostile glance at Judas who averted his eyes. "Whatever the hell that is. Let the priests and the pharisees and the scribes worry about the authenticity of his lineage—descendant of David or not, who cares? Because we—the children of Israel—who've been pushed off our land, who've been murdered and enslaved, who've been raped and starved and crucified couldn't care less."

"He also healed the sick."

Reuben reached across the table and grabbed Judas by his tunic. "We need a messiah who's a warrior or a revolutionary prophet or, at the very least, a good brigand chief—not a doctor!"

"Settle down—both of you." Dinah plunked the bottom of the clean cup on the table in order to disrupt the intensity of their tempers. "I hope you two—"

"Not now," Reuben said through clenched teeth. "Not now."

But she stubbornly waited until Reuben released Judas's tunic. Then she poured wine into both cups before leaving their table.

Reuben picked up his full cup and took a drink as he studied Judas's tormented eyes. "If he wanted to be elected a king, he should have approached the ruling class where it might have made a difference."

Judas grunted. "No. Not against Herod." He grabbed his cup and drank deeply.

"See? You admit it yourself." Reuben set his cup down and leaned against the table toward Judas. "He'd cut us to pieces within a day if any of us revealed our loyalty to your Jesus."

"But we need a leader. We need a centralized authority. We need political power. Not brigand chiefs attacking Roman baggage trains in the countryside or rebels terrorizing priests in the streets of Jerusalem; and not the cry of protest over Rome and its evils against us as our only cause to rally on."

"That'll never happen." Reuben shook his head. "It's hopeless. Yahweh is our only true King of Israel."

"Nobody disputes that. Not even Jesus."

"And yet, I suppose he said Yahweh proclaimed him to be the Messiah—the anointed king from the House of David."

Judas's voice dropped to a whisper. "He proclaimed he was the son of man."

"What was that? Speak up."

"He's the son of man!—he says."

"Ridiculous crap. I'd like to see that title presented for popular election."

"I told you: he had a following."

"But would they have supported strike and run warfare against Rome?" Reuben watched Judas scratch his face. "I see you hesitate."

"As you know, he spoke only of peace and love."

"A ploy, you think? I mean—really, I ask you."

"I don't know." Judas gulped down some of his wine. "I honestly don't know." He turned away from Reuben in an effort to suppress his agitation.

"Bah, this Jesus of yours has always made me nervous. He confused the issues at hand. He confused the people—even those among us. You, for instance."

"I deny nothing. But *you* join that group and see if *you* can do better."

"It's too late for that and you know it. But I almost wish I had."

"Then you would have been another one among us subjected to the gaze in his eyes, the tone in his voice, the gentleness of his touch."

"You almost speak of him as a woman."

"It's difficult to speak of him at all."

"Look, Judas, try to save yourself. Do your best with what's left of his followers. We need supporters. There simply aren't enough men or weapons. Surely there are some among his band with the resources and the willingness to fight against this Roman oppression—now that they've lost their leader."

"Willing? Perhaps. Resources? Maybe. Brave enough? Well, that's another story."

Reuben snatched his cup off the table with disgust. "What a waste. All this popularity he's generated for himself and for what?"

Judas waited for Reuben to finish drinking his wine. "He's certainly not your usual prophet."

Reuben carelessly set his cup back onto the table. "If he was one at all."

"He was anointed by that other prophet, John."

"And he lost his head for it—good." Reuben noted that Judas was stricken with horror by that last remark. "Don't worry, Judas, we've plenty of prophets in Palestine. There's one under every rock, it seems. But messiahs, well, that in itself is a revolutionary act. And since Jesus proclaimed himself a king—hmm, well—see how expendable he became?" Reuben stood up prepared to leave.

"Where are you going?"

"To spread the word about our dying King of Israel. That should continue to piss off both Rome and Herod and scare up more of the landless to join us."

"But that will get many of us arrested."

"For heaven's sake, Judas, what do you think we're doing? We're all trying to start a revolt—no matter how hopeless it is—" Reuben pointed toward the open window. "He was expendable: he knew that. He at least earns my respect for his bravery." He peered at Judas with a set of hard eyes. "Expendable. All of us are. Understand that and you'll lose your fear."

"But—"

"We'll talk more later." Then Reuben experienced a sudden revelation. "You know, we've got to get you before the Sanhedrin, somehow."

"Oh, is that so?" Judas replied, his sarcasm slurred by his excess wine consumption.

"You know more about this man than any of us."

"Seeing them would serve no purpose. Besides, I've already tried. They wouldn't see me."

"But their servants and assistants would. Perhaps even a scribe or two. Their words would certainly reach the inner courts."

"For what purpose?" Judas picked up his cup and gulped down the rest of his wine. The final amount of wine seemed to blur his vision. "He's dying on the wood as we speak."

"If he's as innocent as you keep telling me, his arrest and execution should serve as an additional way of causing more unrest and maybe increase our enrollment."

Judas slammed his cup on the table encouraged by what he just heard. "Those were my thoughts exactly!—at one time. But not according to Ganto."

Reuben leaned over the table close enough to Judas to smell his bad breath. "Maybe all is not lost. If we play this right, we could instigate a flurry of riots in the lower city that could spread into the upper city. Who knows, it could eventually go beyond the city walls—perhaps through the Damascus Gate toward Golgotha itself."

"That could get a lot of people hurt."

"The hell with them. Serve those ghouls right for enjoying the suffering of men under Roman torture." Reuben straightened up and took a single step away from Judas.

"But—"

"Judas, Judas." He shook his head. "Something's not right within you."

"I know it must be obvious."

"And dangerous. There are those among us who are beginning to wonder where your allegiance lies. Truly."

Judas twisted his mouth into a cynical frown. "And not you, I suppose."

Reuben tapped his chest with both hands to demonstrate his innocence. "I swear it."

"You couldn't convince a Syrian."

"For the love of God, it's the truth."

"For the love of your own skin, you mean. Go on. Get out of here. You're just like the rest. And I saw Simeon scurrying out of here earlier."

"But Judas, I swear—"

"Shall I throw a cup at you, too?" Judas focused a vicious pair of eyes on Reuben. "A man's got to do what a man's got to do."

The intensity of Judas's eyes managed to have a painful effect on Reuben's own eyes. He backed away from Judas until he reached the entrance leading out into the street. Then he waited for Judas to avert his eyes and release him from whatever frightening power Judas suddenly had over him. As soon as Judas buried his face within his cradled arms on the table, Reuben scrambled out of the tavern and collided into Simeon.

"What happened?" Simeon demanded.

"Let's get out of here."

Simeon followed Reuben, who was walking at a quick pace. "Wait up. I saw you with Judas."

"And he saw you."

Simeon caught up to him. "And what did he say?"

"Nothing we didn't already know."

"Then we're found out," Simeon said. "We're all doomed."

"Let's just say that Judas is aware he's operating alone."

"Worse. He's an outcast. That will certainly lead to desperation."

Reuben directed Simeon into a narrower street. "What's the matter with you? Didn't you see his face when he came in?"

"Of course. He looked as if he'd seen a ghost."

"He smells of death. I'll not have anymore to do with him."

"On what basis?"

Reuben stopped walking and turned to Simeon. "Basis?"

"What shall we say is the basis for our disassociation with him? What do we tell the others?"

"Contaminated. Untrustworthy. A potential informer."

"That's the worst accusation of all."

Reuben leaned against a wall, feeling exhausted. "And to start now is better than later."

"You really sense something, don't you?" Simeon said feeling uneasy.

A shadow cut Reuben's face on a diagonal. "I sense death. No. I saw it in his eyes."

"Should we warn Ganto?"

"Of course, stupid. We'll tell him everything."

"Then that means—"

"Yes. Another execution, maybe."

Simeon started walking away from Reuben. "I'll not have anything to do with this."

"You'd better. If word should reach Ganto that we withheld any information from him—"

"You!" Simeon wheeled around and planted himself in the middle of the narrow street. "You're the one who spoke with him. Not me!"

Reuben pushed himself away from the wall and approached Simeon. "You piece of shit. He'd kill both of us anyway."

"Then . . . then all is lost."

"Not if I have anything to do about it." Reuben nudged Simeon on the shoulder and began walking. "Come on."

"Where are we going?"

"I think I know where to find Ganto."

"This is no good, Reuben. I'm telling you it feels no good."

"Shut up and grow a set of balls between your legs. We haven't any choice. We haven't. It's him or us."

Judas raised his head from the table, his eyes blurred with tears, his demeanor saturated with wine. "I did not betray him. I did not betray him. I did not betray him!"

Dinah broke away from the two groups of men after communicating to them that she still wanted to be left undisturbed with that drunken lout. She quickly approached Judas, leaving her duties with her assistant, Lila, once again. "What are you doing? You are calling much too much attention to yourself."

Judas scanned the large room and assessed the forced disinterest of its occupants. "All they care about is their wine and hard dicks and the spectacle of death."

Dinah sat on the stool adjacent to him. "You can't always count on that."

Judas lowered his head until the flat of his forehead met the table top. "People keep putting words into my mouth. I said nothing to them about Jesus; neither to Herod's police nor to Pilate's legionnaires."

"You told me yourself you bribed a centurion."

"He was already ordered to arrest my Master."

"You're ... " Dinah cleared her throat. "You ... you also told me that you kissed him last night, just moments before his arrest."

"That was to prevent any violence against him, I told you." Judas's voice deflated steadily until its tone rang hollow. "I ... I was protecting him from the Roman sword—from that damn centurion who already knew we were at Gethsemane."

"The sword would have been a merciful end." Dinah shuddered. "From Gethsemane to Golgotha. You should have used the sword on him yourself."

"I had a dagger hidden under my cloak."

"Too bad you didn't have the courage to use it."

"How was I to know?" He raised his head again, revealing a set of wild eyes. "I should have used the hidden dagger on myself when I was given this purse of silver."

"Yes, I know, a heavy purse—I can see."

"There were thirty full-weighted pieces!"

Dinah pressed her right forefinger across Judas's lips. "Not so loud, you fool. There are many hidden daggers in this room—all without a conscience, I can assure you. Any one of them would slit your throat for even a tenth of what's left in your purse."

"Then show them," Judas said with contempt. "Go ahead, tell them. What do I care?" His eyes crossed with somberness. "By my own hand or one of theirs—I'll not be long among the living, I can assure you." He studied the preoccupied patrons at the tavern's window with increased venom. "Look at them, the ghouls. Didn't you tell me that one of them on that hill was your man?"

"I did."

"Then how can you stand that . . . that show?"

"You don't see me standing by the window, do you? Besides, in my own way, keeping business as usual is my form of tribute to him. Azriel would have been pleased."

"Azriel." Judas chuckled cruelly. "He's beyond anything called pleasure at this moment."

Dinah picked up the cup of wine and dashed what was left of it into Judas's face. "I'll not take that from anybody—especially you."

"Way to go, Dinah!" one of the men shouted.

Dinah stood up. "Shut up, Gilgal!" She almost threw the cup at him.

The biggest man among them slapped Gilgal on the back of the head to encourage him to stay out of Dinah's business.

"I did not betray him, I said."

"So you've said." She looked down at Judas. "And so you say."

Judas picked up the purse from the table and offered it to her. "I do. And . . . and I'm sorry. Go on, take my purse."

"You're becoming pathetic. I'll not touch it for any more than you drink or . . . or for whatever other services you require."

Judas dropped the purse back on the table and shook his head. "Even a harlot is more honest than I."

"You give yourself too much credit. Besides, I'm no longer directly engaged in that profession." Dinah sat back down and leaned against the table to get close to him. She spoke suggestively. "But still, in your case, I think I could make this an exception, you know, in offering you another way that I might earn more of that silver."

Judas studied her while suspended in a cold, penetrating silence. "You don't want to satisfy me. You want to satisfy your own hope."

"About what?" she said innocently.

"Nothing can help them. Nothing."

Laughter interrupted them along with an open declaration from one of the men standing at the window, which ignited an open conversation that caught Judas's and Dinah's attention:

"The truth of the matter is, Jesus seemed to be a likable enough fellow."

"With a number of strange ideas."

"No question about that. But this is a land full of prophets with strange ideas. So much so that Rome doesn't even take note."

"In religious matters, that's true. Rome cares not a whit about God."

"Our God. Nor our opinions."

"Only in our taxes."

"This is true. It always has to do with money."

"And politics."

"That's right. That prophet has been accused of being a king. That makes him a leader—and in Rome's eyes—a leader of a band of insurgents."

"There are lots of those about."

"And there have been lots of entertaining crucifixions as a result."

"Hmm. Another messiah among us that bites the dust. Dinah, more wine, please. We need to drink a toast for another lost king of the Jews."

Several of the men laughed.

Dinah peered at her assistant, Lila—the glance from Dinah was enough to convey her order. Lila picked up a serving pitcher of wine and took it to the men at the window, where she refilled their cups.

Judas dropped his head, face down, into his arms, which were cradled before him on the table. It looked as if he had passed out, so Dinah left him for a while in order to tend to her business.

The men at the tavern this hour were consuming an unusually large volume of wine, forcing her to take down three of her empty wine skins on her way to the storage room in order to provide the necessary serving pegs she needed to accommodate the full skins of wine she planned to hang in their place. Since the goat skins were large and quite heavy, she had to carry them from the storage room and hang them onto the serving pegs behind her tavern's long bench, one at a time. The chore made her wheeze a little, but she didn't mind this routine task. Obviously, she could have directed her assistant to take the burden of wine resupply, but Lila was much younger and prettier than she and that was good for business. Wine flowed from her tavern's pitchers more frequently with a pretty face and an attractive figure tending to it; a firm rump, willing to be freely slapped, didn't hurt either.

Dinah managed to catch her breath by the time Judas began to stir from his lifeless position. She quickly went over to him and helped him up from his stool. Then she made sure Lila had everything under control before she led him into her back room.

Nearly running the length of the room's wall opposite from the doorway they passed through, sat a couch of Roman design: a four-legged wooden frame with arms at both ends and straps interwoven across the top to support an unbleached cotton mattress stuffed with straw. A pillow was propped against the arm at one end, with a folded woolen blanket at the other end. Beside the head of the couch and sitting flush against the adjacent wall in front of a small open-shuttered window, stood a wooden storage chest, which also served as a side table for the empty goblet upon it. And parallel to the couch's foot, there was a small oil vessel and a clay lamp sitting lifelessly among the shadows within a niche in the wall.

"You've so much furniture," Judas noticed, despite his wine-soaked stupor. "A couch? Why? Business goes so well? How can you afford this? And your tavern—how?"

Dinah guided him to the couch. "Sit down before you fall down."

Judas continued to scan the room after he was seated near the edge of the couch. There was a large empty basin and an egg-shaped jug full of water beside it; both were sitting on the floor to the right of the niche and nestled in the corner.

"My man, Azriel, said: If a Roman can sit and lie above the floor to sleep and drink, so can Galileans and Judeans. That's partly why my tavern does such good business."

"You mean, tables and stools?" He tossed his purse of silver on the couch.

"Partly. It's no secret that my tavern caters to laborers and craftsmen, to rogue Syrian mercenaries and bandits, and to the poor fugitive with a stolen talent or two. I accept any form of payment as well: copper, silver, bronze— Roman, Greek, Jewish, Tyrian—no matter, a denarii is the same as a shekel to me. I've been known to exchange wine for a sack of corn or beans or lentils. No fair exchange is improper to me."

"And you say you run a good business."

"I try."

"But still—how?"

"My man set me up after one of his most successful raids against a large and heavily laden Roman pack train."

Judas stood up as if he were going to leave. "He's another bandit leader?"

Dinah pushed him backward. "Sit down, you idiot. You're safe here. Besides, he wouldn't have done you any harm—nor will any of his old band of men. He's—he was—one of us."

"I'm no common bandit."

"You're a disciple to a rebel. And in Rome's eyes that makes you equal to a mere bandit."

"My Master spoke of peace and love."

"So did my man." Dinah sat on the couch beside Judas. "Though, he covered up the true meaning of his words with a constant roar of curses." She allowed a degree of sentiment to leak out. "He was a real lion. He wanted me to sit on a stool and drink at a table and sleep above the ground. It's not fair."

"What?"

"That men like him usually end up hanging on the wood. To think, at this very moment, he's dying alongside your rabbi."

"But he's innocent of any wrongdoing."

"Nobody's innocent. And nobody deserves to die in that manner."

"I tried to save him last night. I don't know why. I kissed him. I kissed him to prevent the legionnaire's sword from striking him. The damn Syrian. They arrested him anyway. And I'm stupid."

"Like I said, nobody's innocent." She shifted more closely to him. "Your rabbi. This . . . this—"

"Jesus. Oh Jesus—"

"Yes, yes, yes. He had a large following?"

After regaining his composure. "Sizable enough."

Dinah anxiously bit her lower lip. "Nothing can help them, you said. Are you sure there aren't any plans for a rescue tonight?"

"Rescue?"

"Yes. I know my man is strong enough to last several days. How about yours?"

"He'll be lucky to last another hour."

"Lucky. Strange choice of words."

"I saw him on the streets—on his way to Golgotha. Weak. He was very, very weak." Judas shook his head. "No. There's no rescue planned."

Dinah's lips trembled. "Why? He might last."

"No. He won't. He doesn't want to. Besides, there's none among them—us—who wish to encourage further violence. That wasn't our rabbi's way."

Dinah stood up with an impatience that camouflaged some of her anger. "Damn it all. There are two other men hanging beside him. What about them?"

"They are lost, as well. You know that."

She cried out in desperation. "One of them is my man!"

"Then why don't you at least stand before your man during his final hour of need?"

Dinah was momentarily stunned into silence. The tone of mockery in Judas's voice had a sobering effect on her. She almost whispered her answer. "Why aren't you?"

"I'm a coward. And, in my own way, I've betrayed him."

"You keep saying that. But how?"

"By intent."

"Deeds are all that matter."

"Explain that to my dreams." Judas bent forward and ran the fingers of both hands through the lower strands of his long hair. "We've left him for the dogs."

"They won't be snapping and snarling at their bloody feet until the third or fourth watch."

"No. I meant Roman dogs." He shook his head in disgust. "My partisans, on one side, my fellow disciples on the other, and the high priest's clan—all—have chosen to turn their backs or hide or simply ignore him since he's apparently not an effective messiah against Rome."

"But you've told me he spoke of peace."

"That's my point," Judas countered impatiently. "Where's the revolution in talk like that? He's not worthy of support and, therefore, not worth saving."

"Then what harm can he be to Rome?"

"Since when does that matter? Your very own words, woman. Pilate hates us all. He needs no excuse to slaughter Jews."

"He's such an animal." Dinah sat down on the couch beside Judas again.

"You still haven't answered my question: why aren't you with him during his final hours?"

"My presence would displease Azriel."

"Think again. Even from the distance of your window, haven't you seen the numbers of women present at Golgotha?"

"That's just another form of humiliation for those three naked, dying men on the wood."

Judas almost laughed. "Those men are far beyond that kind of shame. Believe me, crucifixion leaves no room for such a luxury."

"Then I hope one of them is providing my man with some sort of comfort. But I doubt it. And what about this man, Jesus? Why—as is obvious—are there so many women among that crowd at Golgotha?"

"Because he treated them as his equals."

"Ha! Imagine that." Her skepticism quickly dissipated. "Really?"

"His closest friend, a woman, is among them."

"And?"

"And nothing. Only—you should be there."

"What good would an old whore do?"

Judas shrugged his shoulders. "I don't know. But you'd be no less clean than his lady friend."

Dinah stiffened with anger. "Don't mock me, Judas."

"I wouldn't. Believe me."

"Go on, then."

"Well." Judas appeared as if he was searching deeply into his memory. "This woman played the harp on the streets of Jerusalem at one time."

"And?"

"And when they met, he forgave her."

"Ha! Just like that!"

"Yeah." Judas snapped his fingers. "Just like that. She became his disciple then and there and . . . and, well, followed him along with the rest of us."

"So, they became lovers?"

"I don't know anything about that. But, well, I can say she was totally devoted to him."

"And he?"

"I told you: she was treated as an equal. In fact, that was an occasional source for argument among some of us."

"Men," Dinah said bitterly.

"He spoke of love to us, but sometimes he expressed his affection toward her with a public kiss."

"This prophet, then," she said thoughtfully, "you say he treated her well?"

"More than well. I do not jest when I say he considered all women at eye level."

Judas the Gentile

Dinah stood up, walked across the tiny room, and leaned against the wall. "Then Rome is killing a true revolutionary."

"He's unlike anybody I've ever known, I'll grant you that."

"But, as you've said—and in your own miserable way—you still attempted to betray him."

"I had no choice. It was for another kind of revolution." Dinah's penetrating stare made him feel uneasy. "I couldn't kill him. And I think Ganto might kill me for betraying his cause for a widespread violent revolt."

"Ah, yes, Ganto: one of our *great* bandit leaders. You idiots. Rome can't be defeated."

"I know that!" Judas stood up, but quickly lost his balance and fell back onto the couch. "I've already told you that even the Sanhedrin wouldn't have anything to do with our plan for an uprising. I did my best to persuade them to ignore Jesus—like Ganto wanted."

"Ahh, Caiaphas' priestly clan—I see. No wonder." Dinah began to pace the full length of the small room. "They had sense enough to know that Israel is too weak to fight Rome, you idiot. And to think, you tried to bribe them with silver."

"Actually, I only approached one young scribe on his way to the inner courts," Judas said in defense.

Dinah stopped her pacing. "You're lucky he didn't turn against you."

"The fact is, he almost laughed at me when I accused my Master of identifying himself as the son of God."

46

She looked at him incredulously. "What in the world did you expect? You overstated your case, you clown. You . . . you—" A fit of laughter seized her. "You made your prophet a clown with such a statement, a lunatic not worth any serious attention."

"They could have at least locked him up."

"Why bother when Rome is here to take care of such men?" She shook her head. "Stupid." And through bitter clenched teeth, "You're . . . so . . . stupid."

"What?"

"Can't you see? Your so-called prophet was not politically important enough for the Sanhedrin to bother with him: neither to support nor to oppose—those are your own words."

"I know, I know, but my intent—"

"Forget about that," she said as she impatiently waved her hand at him. "Rome governs us. Rome condemns us. Rome nailed him and my man to the wood like the common criminals they are in Pilate's eyes!"

Judas attempted to justify himself once again. "I kissed him last night. I swear, I swear I kissed him to protect him from the Roman sword. But that centurion knew who it was he came for. Our whereabouts were common knowledge."

"Your rabbi should have had the sense to be afraid."

"Oh, he was. He truly was. But we were blind to it by his constant reassurance and his comforting presence. My God, most of them—like children—couldn't even keep their eyes open long enough to pray with him last night."

"Seder wine and a full stomach often do that."

"I heard them coming and ran into the dark to deflect their approach. But the centurion knew the place—and knew the face I kissed with my allegiance; it provided no defense, no protection."

"What did you seriously expect?"

"Well, I told him I'd double the amount."

"Then he was the one you paid the five silver pieces."

"But I had made another transaction with him."

"You bribed him."

"Of course."

"To arrest your master."

"Yes."

"Because of Ganto."

"Yes. And for the cause—the first time."

Dinah leaned closer to him. "The first time."

"Yes."

"Against—"

"Jesus—yes!"

"Ahh, of course." Dinah jabbed her right finger into his chest. "You think like a gentile, Judas."

"I was born in Corinth, so what. I'm a Jew, now."

Dinah began to toy with him. "So, let's see. Don't tell me—you changed your mind and offered him more silver not to arrest your ... your Jesus."

"Double."

Dinah looked down at him with contempt. "Double. You pitiful piece of dung. You don't know what you're doing or what you want. You're dangerous. You're unfit. No wonder you feel so sick with self-contempt. What manner of guilt is this? What manner of man are you that can change from life to death and back? You're no better than an uncircumcised dog—no—an uncircumcised Roman dog."

Judas stood up seething with anger. "There's a limit to what I'll take—especially from a whore."

Dinah backed away. "At least I know who I am—a child of Israel who can bathe herself clean with soap and water."

"Stop it, I say."

"But you—your filth arises from the blood of your own kind. Get out!"

"What?"

"You're no use to me, get out!"

"Why vent your anger at me for their suffering? As we've agreed: they were arrested by Roman legionnaires, condemned by a Roman prosecutor, and crucified by Roman guards."

Despite Judas's appeal, Dinah was unreasonably relentless—perilously out of control. She peered at him with scorn. "Gentiles. None of our people would be crucified if it weren't for Greeks and Romans. Even your precious master would have disappeared within the multitudes and would have been forgotten in time to become, once again, the dust of Israel. Gentile." She spat at Judas. "The scourge of Palestine."

Judas's anger exploded in a murderous fury. Realizing she had crossed over the line, Dinah began to back away. But not soon enough to avoid Judas's lunge toward her.

He pinned her against the wall opposite the couch, grabbed her by the throat, and began to strangle her in earnest. "You whore! You discard! You embarrassment to the Law of Moses! How dare you throw Judean superiority at me!"

Dinah struggled desperately against Judas's mounting rage and the complementary increase in the pressure of his hands that checked her breathing. Within a short passage of time, her large dark eyes became wide with terror and panic over her mortally dangerous situation. She finally managed to punch him on the right temple, knocking his brimless cap off his head.

The impact of the blow forced him to release her throat and stagger backward. "I . . . I deserve to be counted." The immediate aftereffect of the blow suddenly intensified. He pressed his hand against his temple. "Damn! You bitch! I deserve to be accepted as a child of Israel."

Dinah was still gasping and wheezing and reaching for her breath. She knew escape was impossible since Judas was standing between her and the doorway. And she knew what was necessary to help diffuse this situation, but her anger was still beyond the control of her rationality. To continue in this manner was suicidal and she knew it—she knew it! But she didn't care. Her man, Azriel, was suffering on the wood this very moment: dying of thirst and misery, of pain and exposure, of hopelessness and abandonment—torture. The thought of his loss was torture. There was nothing she could do—nothing!—but lash out at this pitiful man before her, who was obviously in as much pain over the loss of his rabbi as she was over her man. In fact, she could see that he was even on the verge of complete madness. So, what was she doing? What was she doing! What manner of suicide was this!? "Convert. You sound like a convert. And by your acquired accent, a Galilean one at that."

"And what of it? My Master is a Galilean."

"And so is mine! But you're not fit to kiss my man's feet. You're not even fit to die in his place, only—God, damn God, if you are there—" She fell to her knees and began to weep. "Save my Azriel from the burden of his suffering." She peered at Judas with contempt. "You lack the strength of a Galilean. My man will suffer on the wood for days. But you, you would have perished easily, you . . . you weak convert with a Judean temperament."

"It's not my fault. It's not—"

"Get out. I've already told you: you're no use to me. Get out. Get out! Get out!"

Judas realized he'd face certain disaster if he stayed in Dinah's company a moment longer. So, he left in a confused state of thoughts mixed with the anxiety of rejection and prejudice. And as he staggered across the length of the tavern to reach the doorway, he realized he was being ignored by the other customers. He glanced over his shoulder and saw Dinah standing at the threshold of her back room's entranceway—the manner in which her arm had partially drawn aside the privacy curtain still obscured the right side of her figure. But it was apparently enough for her patrons to see that she was unharmed.

Once outside the tavern, he stumbled along the road leading toward the city gate. His destination was as uncertain as his future and his mood as dark as the approach of the first watch of a new day. And yet, there was a destination: it was away—away from Golgotha. Not much of a destination. Not much of anywhere, really. He was a coward. Too cowardly to stand before him. Too ... too ...

He felt a deep penetrating chill. It made him shiver. And as he continued to walk, he began to feel soggy: it had begun to rain—thunder and lightning assaulted him from a dark threatening sky. The ground beneath him seemed to tremble, but he knew this physical distortion came from his own present state of misery. He could trust in nothing, nobody, not even his own senses.

He went to his right and leaned against the city's wall as soon as he passed through the gate. The house he was facing helped to form the beginning of a narrow alley, which ran between the stone-walled residences and the city's wall—its continued length disappeared into the growing darkness.

He trembled with the land as he labored against the suffocation he experienced by the nearness of the wall opposite him. The fluidity of his surroundings made him feel as if he could have touched the wall in front of him and actually push it away so he could breathe better. But then, what would have been the point? What, if anything, mattered?

Suddenly, he heard something to his right. He turned his head and squinted in that direction, trying to pierce the darkness in order to increase his visual distance. Several figures finally appeared. They became clearer and clearer as they approached him, until he finally recognized one of them: Ganto! Unfortunately, he was recognized in return.

"There he is—after him!"

Judas bolted to his left and out through the city gate onto the main road leading toward Golgotha.

"Come back here, you traitor!" one of them shouted.

"What happened to the silver!?" cried another.

Judas began to run harder—he realized he'd left the silver on the couch. He heard their gaining footsteps behind him.

CHAPTER 2
Random Time, Random Place: Judean Women

They knew each other all their lives; had greeted each other at the local well each morning and evening, where they had come to collect fresh water for their family's daily needs a countless number of times. This was one of the welcomed chores, among the many that were not so welcomed, around the household. And it was one of the few times they were able to venture outside of their homes. At that precise moment, however, the meeting at the well was a small disappointment, since, aside from one other woman, this social center was without much activity or gossip.

Rachel recognized Lilith hauling up her ladling bag by its long rope. Lilith was older than she, more conservative: she kept her upper mantle draped across her face almost all the time.

"Hello there, Lilith," said Rachel with her bright and youthful quality—her mantle draped loosely over her head and shoulders. She lowered her large clay jug from her head and set it on the ground beside the well along with her own leather ladling bag, rope, and small cushion.

Lilith raised her head from its bent position, but she continued hauling up her ladling bag. "I dislike this time of year."

"But, Lilith, it's the Passover season."

"And Jerusalem is crowded to a standstill with pilgrims."

Rachel sat near the mouth of the well. "My husband is delighted by the prosperity."

Lilith rested her full ladling bag on the edge of the well. "For whom?"

"Look at the smoke," Rachel said as she indicated the city's atmosphere by raising her arm upward. "Everywhere there are lambs being roasted."

"And everywhere I cannot breathe from the bitter stench."

Rachel watched Lilith pour the water from her ladling bag into her clay jug. "A small price to pay."

"And I'd gladly pay it if there was something left to buy at the markets."

"I admit you have to get there early to get good fruit and bread."

Lilith lowered her ladling bag into the well again. "That's an understatement. And what about the doubled prices?"

"It's Passover."

"Right." She started hauling up her full ladling bag again. "We were liberated from Egypt to be robbed by merchants."

"Don't be so hard, Lilith. This is Nisan and it's a beautiful day."

"And I'm being practical," she said as she poured more water into her jug.

Rachel stared off into the distance. "I fear there are too many of us who think that way this time of year."

"Now you're being pious."

"No wonder there's so much tension in the air during this season."

"Don't worry," Lilith said as she inspected her ladling bag, "Pilate is good at dealing with disturbances."

"Lilith!"

"It's true and you know it. Damn. The wooden cross brace in my bucket is about to break."

"Here, use mine." Rachel picked up her ladling bag as she shuddered. "He's a cruel and sadistic beast."

"He's a man like any other."

"A pagan." Rachel offered her ladling bag to Lilith.

"Our people rule no better—especially during hard times. No thank you dear, I've enough water." Lilith stepped away to allow Rachel to fetch her own water. "I've never heard of a Herod or a priest cutting back on taxes."

"You speak like a man." Rachel positioned her jug upright and against the wall of the well and uncoiled her rope. "These are not matters for us to discuss."

"I'll say what I please when it affects my purse."

Rachel lowered her ladling bag into the well as Lilith coiled her rope. "You'll not corrupt me."

"You're no better than a donkey in a stable."

"How dare you." Rachel held her rope more as if she were fishing than about to haul up water.

"Since you act like property, you might as well be compared to property."

"I'll not be called an ass by you or anyone."

Lilith threw up her hands in despair. "You're hopeless." Their silence and sudden inactivity remained strong. "And . . . and I'm sorry. Really."

Rachel started hauling up her water. "That's better."

Lilith began to inspect her ladling bag. "Yes, I'm going to have to pay a carpenter to repair this bucket." She peered at Rachel from the corner of her eye, then continued her attempt to change the subject and, therefore, the mood between them. "But say, what do you think of this man, Jesus?"

Rachel waited until she poured her first bag of water into her jug. "Well, he seems to be far different from the one that was called the Baptizer."

"There's absolutely no doubt about that, Rachel. John the Baptizer was like a beast: always hollering at the top of his lungs."

"A bit like you I would say."

"Rachel, please, I said I was sorry."

"Only teasing." Rachel lowered her ladling bag into the well. "He smelled like a camel, too—or so they say."

They both laughed.

"Yes. He was a bit too frightening." Lilith sat on the mouth of the well opposite Rachel.

"But that was not a good reason for his execution."

"I didn't say it was—nor was it the true reason."

"I know, I know. I'm just concerned over what reasons will be used against Jesus."

"You like him, don't you?"

Rachel set her full ladling bag near the edge of the well. "I'd be lying if I didn't say he interests me."

"Be careful, Rachel. Judging by his activities, he's destined for a bad end—and soon. I can feel it."

Rachel lifted her bag and began pouring the water into her jug. "His eyes are soft and his speech is soothing. What can be wrong with that?"

"Nothing. But it's what he sees and what he says that matters. Not how. Rome will eventually classify him a revolutionary, if they haven't already. And anybody associated with him, directly or indirectly, will find themselves in deep trouble when Pilate's patience runs thin."

"What patience?" Rachel tossed her ladling bag back into the well. "That man is without patience."

"All the worse."

"He hates us."

"It's very possible that nobody has brought Jesus to his attention."

"You mean, one prophet among several?"

"That's right. They seem to be coming out from under a multitude of rocks lately."

"And not a woman among them, either."

"Rachel!"

"What?"

"You speak too freely."

"I speak my mind—like you."

"Well, it'll be safer to keep your mind here at the well—and between you and me."

"I'll not be afraid of ideas."

"I hope you are aware where most of these prophets have ended up."

"You mean, how." Rachel pulled on her rope with the energy of irritability behind it. "I'm no fool!"

"However you prefer to say it, dead is dead: whether by crucifixion or stoning, by the lash or the executioner's broad sword."

Rachel poured the water straight into her jug and tossed the ladling bag back into the well. "This one is different."

"No matter. His prophetic preaching is a challenge to their authority."

"To our priests, you mean."

"Between you and me, to all men. But officially, a challenge to the power of Rome, as well. Haven't you been listening to our men speak? There's no separation between the powers of Herod and Rome."

"Still, even my husband says that Jesus is a prophet of oracles, not of action." Rachel began pulling on her rope to raise her last ladling bag of water. "Rome has nothing to fear from him."

"There's no question about that, my dear. But does he have sense enough to fear Rome?"

"They'll simply dismiss him as a raving lunatic—I hope."

"As should you." She waited until Rachel finished fill-ing her jug. "As should you, I said."

"He's not, you know. I've seen him. I've heard him my-self. I think I like him."

"Ahh. All this talk of deliverance and such makes me nervous. Jerusalem is riddled with fanatics."

Rachel sat on the edge of the well and began coiling her rope. "Maybe. But he hasn't pronounced judgment against anybody as John the Baptizer did. It almost served him right to lose his head over politics."

"Rachel! What a horrible thing to say. Now who speaks like a man?"

"I said almost. And it's the truth."

"The truth. What is truth? If I remember correctly, the Baptizer never preached or offered to lead a riot in the city."

"But Herod probably thought he was going to. Besides, he was openly against our aristocratic priests—not just Herod's second marriage. It wouldn't have taken much to incite King Aretas into enough anger to send an invasion force into Palestine. Think about it. How would your fa-ther feel if you'd been discarded like Herod's first wife? No—the Baptizer might not have wanted to lead a revolu-tion, but his politics was close to starting a war between Aretas and Herod. His head had to come off to silence him."

Lilith shook her head. "Rachel, Rachel. You're listen-ing much too hard."

"Well, all I can say is Jesus is not playing politics with Herod."

"No, worse! With Rome."

"Enough already, Lilith."

"Please, don't get angry with me again."

"I'm not angry!"

A short silence separated them momentarily.

Lilith stood up before Rachel. "Well, all I can say is, you've been warned."

"That's right." Rachel hooked her ladling bag onto her left arm. "I've been warned." She lifted her jug and balanced it on the small thin cushion that she had just placed on her head.

"And when they find you in bed with him, they'll show you no mercy."

"Enough, Lilith," Rachel said heatedly. "I've washed his feet once. That's all."

Lilith's jaw dropped. "Washed—umm, umm, umm— that's enough." She raised her own jug to her head.

"No. This is enough, thank you. I need to get back home." Rachel stormed away without looking back or verbally responding to Lilith's entreaties.

"I'm sorry, Rachel. I'm sorry." She stood there until she was sure Rachel wasn't going to respond to her call, then turned away in the opposite direction to go home.

CHAPTER 3

The First Watch: Bandits, Rebels, and Thieves

Heavy rain pelted Judas in the face as he ran into the thunder and lightning. Everything seemed to be against him: even the hostile night's sky wouldn't allow him to vanish into its darkness.

They caught up to him before he could disappear among a grove of trees. At first, Judas felt a single hand tugging the back of his tunic, then his legs caved in from the impact of somebody tackling him on his right side. He tumbled sideways into a helpless roll, which abruptly ended with him on the flat of his back, where he was breathless and aching and pinned hopelessly to the ground by several men. When he opened his eyes, a huge figure was standing over him.

"Somebody uncover a burning lamp," the figure said.

"It's too dangerous for that, Ganto," one of the other men said.

"A feeble glow at this distance will be harmless, especially among these trees. Come on, damn it! I must see his face before I slit his throat." Somebody handed Ganto an uncovered oil lamp. The glow illuminated his formidable presence. Ganto quickly cupped one of his hands over the flame to protect it from the wind and rain.

Life had tempered Ganto's iron hard body and his sharp disposition into a fearless warrior as well as a capable brigand chief. As a man of anger, he was not to be trifled with; and as a born leader, he was a man best left unchallenged.

Ganto wore a short, knee-length, half-sleeved tunic made of a coarsely woven wool that was tied to his waist with a twice-wrapped linen sash. Leather shoes protected his feet and a hidden dagger protected his life. Just above his hard piercing eyes there was a bleached linen cloth wrapped several times around his cap-covered head, forming a turban. His facial hair was full and thick, his voice deep, and his hairy limbs muscular. To his enemies, his stout and brutish appearance masked his deep sense of justice as well as his empathy for the countless poor and hungry peasants of Palestine. To these oppressed people, men of his kind served as a model of strength, as well as a flesh and blood reality on which to anchor their hope.

Ganto lowered the lamp to Judas's frightened face.

"Ganto, please, have mercy on me," Judas pleaded.

"You worm. Did you really think you were going to get away from me?"

"I . . . I didn't know."

"Didn't know what?"

"That I had any reason to run from you."

Ganto took the lamp away from Judas's face with disgust. He decided he didn't like the expression he saw and struck Judas on the cheek with the back of his hand. "Then what were you doing a moment ago, you liar?"

"Dathan told me—and Reuben—yes! They said I was in danger—and not very long ago, either."

"Get this piece of shit on his feet," Ganto ordered. "Dathan!"

"Yes, Ganto . . . yes."

Ganto waited until his men assisted Judas to his feet. "Did you speak to this worm today?"

"I told you I did—at Dinah's. But I didn't warn him about anything."

Judas struggled against the two men, who held him firmly in place. "You liar!"

"I swear, Ganto. He barely shared his cup of wine with me."

"And what about Reuben?"

"He . . . he was with Simeon, I think," Dathan whined.

"So, where are they?" Ganto demanded.

"Probably . . . probably looking for you!"

"If you're lying, you little worm—"

"Why should I?"

"And the silver?"

"I saw his purse on the table," Dathan said. "I swear."

"There's no purse on him now, Ganto," said one of the men who held Judas in place.

"The young scribe I met with at the outer court of the Gentiles wouldn't take it."

Ganto pressed his right fist into his left hand. "So, you decided on a drinking binge for yourself, instead."

"I left it behind," Judas said. "I forgot it."

Ganto struck him again. "Now I know you're lying. Nobody forgets that much silver no matter how strong the drink."

"I left it on Dinah's couch!"

"You?" Ganto erupted with a mean and guttural chuckle. "And Dinah? She wouldn't allow a dog on her couch."

"They were sitting together at a table," Dathan said on Judas's behalf.

"I'll not bother Dinah this night. Her man is dying on the wood."

"But she has it," Judas said. "She has it."

"Shut up!" Ganto handed the lamp to one of his men. "Go to Dinah's. You know what to do. If she has what's left of it, then the purse is safe enough. And if not—" He glared at Judas. "Bring him along."

"Help!"

"Gag him," Ganto ordered.

"Let's hang him here and now and be done with it."

"Do as I say and bring him along. There's a friendly herdsman close by who can be trusted." Ganto suddenly heard footsteps approaching them. "Your daggers, quick! Cover that lamp."

Except for those who held Judas prisoner, the lot of them crouched in a defense posture with their weapons drawn.

"Ganto. Ganto, is that you?" The intruder uncovered a flickering lamp. "There's nothing to fear. It's me, Balak."

The tension among Ganto's men quickly dissipated into a cascade of nervous laughter.

"Damn you, Balak, I could ring your neck," said Ganto.

"Word got to me late that you had given orders to assemble." Balak raised his lamp in order to get a better look at the prisoner. "That's right. He's the one."

"One what?"

"My family starved because of him, Ganto."

"But he's been one of us for quite some time."

"Then why the restraining men?"

"That's another matter," Ganto said.

"Well, it's true that I'm fairly new to this band." Balak exposed his own crude dagger and approached Judas. "But he's the one, alright."

"Put that away," Ganto ordered.

"But—"

"I said put it away unless you want to feel the metal of my own blade ripping through your side."

Balak reluctantly tucked his knife inside his tunic. "All I want is justice."

"Remove Judas's gag," Ganto commanded.

"I've never seen you before," Judas blurted as soon as the gag was clear of his mouth.

Balak approached him with pure hatred. "That's because you never took your eyes off your scrolls as you reached out for the amount I could pay you."

"Was it enough?" Judas asked hopefully.

Balak spat on the ground near Judas's feet. "It was never enough, publican. Not when it came to increasing the weight of your own purse."

"I . . . I had to make a living."

"Robber. Murderer."

"I'm . . . I'm sorry."

"It's too late for that."

"But I'm one of you, now. I've been so for a long while."

"Never long enough to wipe away the wrongs you've done to me and countless others." Balak looked at Ganto with eyes that revealed the pain of his suffering and the advanced age that had caused the heavy gray in his hair and the constant tremor of his thin limbs. His tunic—almost a rag—was in worse condition than Dathan's. "I don't care what this one has done against our band or our cause or any other injustice he's probably guilty of. I only care about what he's done to my—our—women and children."

"Not to mention our dignity," Dathan added.

"Right. He's taken that with our land and our homes, to be sure."

"Then what are we waiting for?" one of the others said. "Let's hang the dog."

"No, wait," Judas shouted. "You don't understand. I'm no longer that man. I'm no longer that tax collector."

"I've heard he held the purse and guided the finances of that Jesus band you assigned him to, Ganto," said another man among them.

Ganto scratched his beard, then grinned. "That's right, Judas. How do you explain that?" He approached Judas.

"Come on, between you and me—" He made a show of whispering into Judas's ear. "I bet you ended up with an extra cup of wine and a few hidden morsels of food by the end of each day."

"Not true! I was fair and equal—"

"Liar! Nobody can change their basic nature so quickly—if at all."

"I'm not the same man, I'm not the same man!"

"That's your tragedy, not mine."

"Hang him," Balak interjected.

"And quickly," Dathan added. "Before something prevents us."

"No, not yet," Ganto said. "I've a better idea."

"Good," said Balak with relish. "I'm for any kind of torture against him before seeing his death."

"No, no," Ganto said. "We'll not act like Romans. No. There's a safe place I know of nearby. Let's take him there where we can leisurely get at the truth."

"The truth! The truth? What is truth?"

"Something that has caught my curiosity on this strange, wet, windblown night."

"It is an eerie night," Balak agreed. "And frightening. The earth seems to be full of unrest."

Ganto snatched the lamp from Balak's hand. "Only children fear the thunder behind the lightning and the rain."

"But the earth—"

"Bah!"

"Balak is right," said Dathan. "This heavy darkness is premature. And the ground seems to grumble."

"You're still on your feet, aren't you? Bah! There are women at Golgotha—Galilean as well as Judean—who are acting more bravely than the lot of you. I'll hear no more of this. Gag him, damn it, and let's go."

Judas fought successfully against the gag as he spoke. "I'll not go down like a lamb in the same way those who chopped down Herod's golden eagle atop of our sacred Temple."

Judas's sudden spark of defiance caught Ganto's interest. "They were courageous, though."

"What? In waiting for their arrest? Sheep."

"We'll not surrender so easily."

"And neither did I to you."

"At least they became respected martyrs."

"Like those nailed to the cross this very moment? You can see how much martyrdom has affected King Herod or Caesar."

"Gag him," Ganto said, having lost his patience with Judas's last remark. "I'll not listen to anymore of this nonsense, right now."

"Then what about him?" Balak inquired.

Ganto scrutinized Judas for effect. "What about him?"

"Well, he's neither a lamb nor a martyr; neither a leopard nor a patriot."

"He's a dog from the foulest trash pit," Dathan said to agitate Balak. "A mongrel who cares for no one or no thing but himself." Dathan enjoyed Judas's attempt to speak through his gag. The effort caused Judas to lose his breath. "See? Even when muzzled, they're always ready to bark untruths—"

"And bite any sensible man," Balak maliciously added as he wiped rain from his eyes with the back of his forearm.

Ganto's patience was growing thin. "Enough of this, already. We're too exposed out here." He peered over his left shoulder. "Toward the eastern side of the city, I know of a loyal herdsman who tends a sheepfold converted into a cattlefold for a variety of livestock—camels and horses, asses and oxen—anything that needs tending."

"Yes, anything," Balak said disdainfully. "Anything, including swine, I hear."

"I don't like the superiority in your voice."

"These unclean herdsman—"

"Are honest, hard-working men. I don't want to hear anything more about this. Aher and his people are loyal. They've placed their lives in jeopardy against Rome for men like us many times—including tonight."

"But still, he . . . he raises—"

"Food we've eaten when we were starving."

"I'm not proud of that."

"You hypocrite. You fight the cruelty of Roman Law and embrace the stupidity of our own."

"But swine are—"

"Food. And this man who herds them is an honorable man." He glared at Balak. "Enough, old man. I'll hear no more from any of you on this matter. First, you fear the night and now . . . bah! I'll not tolerate any more of your prejudices."

"But—"

"Another word and you'll be alone in this stormy countryside or roaming the filthy streets tonight." Ganto winked at one of the others. "If you're lucky, somebody will slit your throat and put you out of your bitter misery."

Balak trembled with horror. "Ganto! I didn't mean anything, really!"

"Then shut up—you too, Dathan—and pay your respects when we enter that man's abode. Come on. I'll not repeat myself. All of you are beginning to make me weary." Ganto did not wait to see or hear any of their responses. He stomped toward the direction of his desired destination in a manner demanding that they follow.

He was not further challenged or questioned. The matter was closed. They hurriedly fell into step behind him, pushing Judas along.

Suddenly, a peel of thunder behind a slash of lightning across the sky caused Dathan to cower and Balak to flinch into the steep angle of the rain.

"But I didn't say anything to make Ganto angry," Dathan said sheepishly as he quickly got back into step.

"Shut up," Balak snapped. "Just shut up."

CHAPTER 4

Random Time, Random Place: Judean Men

They picked their way along the vacant narrow street, stepping carefully but unavoidably stepping into refuse and waste, rotting fruit and diluted puddles of urine. The stench of decaying garbage was everywhere and, with nothing but the encroaching darkness to stimulate their senses, the stench became a formidable presence.

Both men looked as if they had fallen on hard times. Not quite beggars, yet, they were living on the edge of starvation as common and unskilled laborers. They were but two among the numerous who scratched an existence in and around Jerusalem. Work was infrequent, if at all, and simple in task: digging refuse ditches, sweeping streets, loading or unloading wagons, clearing rock slides from the Roman roads, anything—anything by the day or the hour to delay the hardships of famine and exposure. If necessary, they resorted to thievery to survive, since their status in Palestinian society made them the moral equals to the criminal element anyway—despite the fact they were once respected members of their rural villages, now taxed or enslaved out of existence by Rome.

Both men were hungry and miserable, barefoot and threadbare—each reduced to a tattered short tunic, a piece of rope for a belt, and a singular dirty rag wrapped and tied around their shaggy heads. Everything else had been sold or traded for food, food, and only food—forget any visits to a barber or the luxury of a bath. Forget anything but today.

"Damn these city dwellers. I'll be happier once we're back in the wilderness."

"And back into greater starvation? Is that really to your liking, Kenah?"

"At least we're safer in the desert."

"Yes, but hungrier." Han spat on a nearby wall. "With increased comfort comes increased danger—so be it."

"Ahh, yes, we live in such comfort."

Han stopped walking. "Don't mock me, Kenah. I'll not roam Peraea again, robbing the tail ends of pack trains or having to beg from shepherds not much better off than I unless . . . unless I absolutely have to. Come on, we've a long way before we reach the northern edge of the lower city."

"Do you know of a place for us to stay in that vicinity?"

"Of course I do, stupid."

They proceeded along a very narrow stone street with the stone walls of residences looming two, sometimes three, stories high. They passed under several arches and occasionally stumbled across a single step leading downward along the street—the general effect was like descending into a great den of filth.

Kenah saw him first. "Wait. Han. Look." He pointed to a body lying face down on the street just ahead. From the attitude of the body and by the knowledge they had gained from their experiences on the streets and in the country-side, there was no doubt that this man was dead.

"What do you think?"

"Probably murder."

"You think?"

"Let's go see what's left."

They approached the body with extreme caution. Han knelt down beside the body, while Kenah stood by as a lookout.

"It's murder, alright. There are several clean knife wounds in his back."

Kenah looked down at the body. "Damn. Was it rob-bery?"

"No, I don't think so. He still has a shepherd's scrip slung over his shoulder."

"Open it!"

Han fumbled with the scrip. "Look here."

"What. What!"

"Several cakes of bread and . . . and dried figs, olives, parched corn, a bit of cheese—even a small flask of wine."

"Bonanza." Kenah threw caution to the wind and knelt beside Han with excitement. "Is there anything else?" He began searching the other side of the body. "Nothing."

"I think I'll take his new sandals."

"No. No articles of clothing. Are you crazy? Somebody might recognize them."

"Good heavens, you're right, Kenah. Sometimes you do have sense." Han stood up. "In fact, let's not be greedy. Let's take the scrip full of food and be gone."

"My stomach agrees with you completely."

As soon as Kenah stood up, they both dashed down to the end of the narrow street, took a right, and zigzagged toward the northern edge of the lower city. And as soon as they felt they had traveled a safe distance away from the unfortunate man lying in the street, they ducked into a very narrow and deserted alleyway, where they found a place to sit with their backs against a wall and the scrip between them.

Han opened the leather bag, took out the flask of wine first, and removed the wooden stopper. "To your health."

"To my thirst, you mean." Kenah licked his lips as he watched Han take the first drink. He was grateful when his turn came.

Then they quietly feasted on the contents of the scrip, savoring every olive, every bite of bread so as not to waste a single hard-won pleasure. Anyone who knew hunger knew to chew their food slowly and carefully and thoughtfully. They shared another drink of wine from the small flask, then began to add talk to the remainder of their meal.

"Do you still think it would have been better to remain outside the city's walls tonight?"

"No." Kenah popped an olive into his mouth and chewed it carefully for a moment before concentrating on its flavor with greater zest.

"But I have to admit," said Han, "it's been a strange-feeling night so far—and all that bad weather, earlier."

"Yeah. Look at us—soaked. And the ground beneath us is no better." Kenah shivered, then leaned to one side and showed Han his wet rear end.

"Agh, get away. I don't know which is worse: more bad weather or your stinking ass."

Kenah lowered his rear end back onto the wet ground. "It's been more than bad weather this night."

"True. Bad people."

"I think truer when you said bad feeling."

"Strange feeling."

"Whatever," Kenah conceded.

"That man, Jesus, sure has his followers upside down with grief and uncertainty."

"Especially his women," Kenah agreed.

"That's true."

"He was an interesting fellow," Kenah mused.

"You mean, strange. But he was no political fool."

"I wouldn't say that, exactly. Look where he is: hanging on a Roman cross."

"Well—I didn't mean that exactly," Han said. "But you sure do have to give him some credit for his bravery. He actually threw the idea of allegiance right back into the faces of several Pharisaic disciples. In fact, he showed elements of a militant warrior."

"I'm not surprised." Kenah belched. "That prophet seemed to be more intelligent than the others."

"Was he! You'll be amused when you hear this. Believe me, I saw and heard this myself. When asked was it lawful to pay taxes to Rome?—he said: 'Give to Caesar the things that are Caesar's.' "

"So?"

"No, no, I'm not telling it right. He asked them to show him a denarius. A denarius. Wasn't that clever? Tiberius's own silver coin."

Kenah scratched his head and shrugged his shoulders. "I . . . I still don't get it."

"You are as dense as a rock, sometimes." Out of habit, Han looked around suspiciously to make sure he was not being watched, then he reached inside his tunic for his hidden purse.

"What are you doing? Say, what's that you have there?"

"A man can't be too careful these days." Han took a coin out of the small purse and placed it on his open palm to display the silver denarius.

"Where did you get that money? Wait. Do you mean to tell me I've been hungry since yesterday and you had this money—"

"There were too many of us yesterday."

"And now?"

"Where do you think we were going before we came upon this evening's treasure."

"Where?"

"To buy something to eat and drink, stupid."

"Really? But . . . but where did you get that purse?"

"Where do you think?" Han deftly wiggled the fingers of his right hand with pride. "I think I've become an excellent pickpocket. But this new skill allows no room for mistakes—or sharing. Although—" Han emptied the other coin from the thin purse. "There was plenty of room for more money in this purse."

"Fine, fine. But what has any of this to do with this prophet Jesus?"

"God, you're a rock. Nothing, really. But here, look. Look at the coin." He offered it to Kenah. "Go on, take it."

"Alright." Kenah carefully squinted at the coin. "I'm looking."

Han slapped him lightly on the shoulder. "Tell me what you see. Describe it for me."

Kenah studied it carefully. "Well. There's a bust of some Roman emperor crowned with a laurel."

"Good. Go on."

"There's an inscription on it."

"Right. And what does it say?"

"You know I can't read."

Han pressed his back against the wall to control his impatience. "It says: 'Augustus son of the Divine Augustus.' "

Kenah looked at the coin and mouthed the words silently to himself. "Oh."

"Turn it over and, again, tell me what you see."

"Another inscription—"

" 'Pontifex Maximus,' go on."

"And . . . and an image of a seated lady."

"The emperor's mother on her divine throne."

The lower corners of Kenah's lips turned downward revealing his perplexity. "Oh."

"Don't you see? Tiberius and his mother are worshipped by these Roman pagans. Their coins are propaganda for their cult. They want us to worship their gods."

Kenah dropped the coin as if it suddenly became red hot in his hand. "I'll have none of that."

Han snatched the coin up from the ground. "Of course not, you idiot. And be a bit more careful. That coin was hard won."

"Sorry."

"It's very easy to lose a coin in a dark alley."

"I said I'm sorry." Kenah's mouth drooped and his gaze remained shallow as he watched Han deposit both coins back into the purse before tucking the purse inside his tunic just above his belt.

Han finally noticed Kenah's blank countenance. "What?"

"Why would this prophet want you to give it back to Caesar?"

"Must I draw you a picture? No, don't answer that. Look, if I asked you whose images and inscriptions you saw on that coin, what would you say?"

"Caesar's—and his mother's."

"Right." Han sidled closer to Kenah with real enthusiasm. "But do you know what he said?"

"If I knew I wouldn't be waiting for your answer."

Han rolled his eyes upward with exasperation. "The drama of any story is wasted on you, I swear. But no matter. I can savor the meaning by myself."

"Does this mean you're not going to finish the story?"

"Alright, alright. Like you, the Pharisee's answer was, 'Caesar's.' And to that Jesus said, 'If you're going to play around with scruples, then you're going to need to look into your own pockets for tainted coins'—you know, Caesar's—'and give back to Caesar what you got from him'—since it's immoral to have it in the first place. See? And then he added: 'Remember, your first allegiance is to God.' Pretty amazing, isn't it?"

Kenah scratched his scraggly beard. "I have to admit, his words sound skillful to me."

"It was a hell of a counterblow if you ask me."

Kenah scratched his head this time—almost as if it hurt. "Yeah, but . . . but what is his political point?"

"What?" Han said irritably.

"I mean: are we not to carry coins?—or not pay tribute to Caesar?—or both?"

It was Han's turn to feel the sting of confusion and display his discomfort with a perplexed countenance. "That's . . . that's not the point."

"Then . . . then what is the point?"

"For God sake, Kenah, you've ruined a perfectly good story."

"Sorry."

"No need to be."

"Maybe—"

"Hold on. Let me think. Let's see: I do know that he pays tribute. He's too much in the public eye to get away with not paying."

"So—"

"Sooo—" Han snapped his fingers. "So. He apparently submits to Rome's tyranny when he pays, but without his verbal endorsement. There. He defies Rome. See?"

Kenah frowned thoughtfully. "That statement seems awfully safe to me—even unclear."

"What do you mean?" Han said impatiently. "Look, since everything in the first place is God's, then Caesar's lordship is less than God's."

"I see. So—"

"So, what's rendered to Caesar can't be worth much."

"Ah. Clever. Yes. Very clear. Now. But—"

"What?"

Kenah searched his mind as if he were trying to rid himself of a headache. "Well, if he had told me this himself, you know, in his own manner, that Caesar's tribute was forbidden, it would have passed me by without notice."

"That's not so very hard to do. Besides, he was speaking to learned men—not to you."

"I . . . I guess."

"There's no guessing about it." Han rolled his eyes in an effort to suppress some of his increasing irritation. "No servant can serve two masters. And since God naturally rules over Caesar—" He shrugged his shoulders to emphasize his inflated smugness.

Kenah scratched his right temple. "Yet, Palestine is still an occupied land."

"Oh, shut up." Han's certainty, along with his lattice-work of rationality seemed to crumble under Kenah's insistent pecking. "Your simplicity is beginning to make me nervous."

"I just thought you understood what that prophet had to say."

"I do—I think. I did—I thought." Han suddenly frowned. "And I'm beginning to believe nobody does."

"But just a moment ago—"

"When under his influence, he seemed to make perfect sense. But when under yours—" Han shook his head in an attempt to clear it. "I refuse to concede that your intelligence is equal to mine."

"I never said it was." Kenah raised both his hands defensively. "I was only asking questions."

Han exploded with anger. "Then it's apparent, then. Alright?!"

"What?" Kenah said softly.

"That I haven't got a straight answer."

"Nor does this prophet, Jesus."

"Maybe not," Han said longingly. "But brother, he sure did sound good when you got close enough to listen to him."

"They say he was a magician."

"His voice was no illusion. Nor were his words or ... or their *apparent* meaning."

"Yeah, yeah. Then what about his ideas?"

"Enough with these damn questions, Kenah. You're beginning to infuriate me!"

Kenah shrunk with timidity. "I'm sorry."

"And enough of your apologies, already." Han stood up and began walking.

"Where are you going?"

"To spend Caesar's money on a few cups of wine."

Kenah stood up, grabbed the empty scrip, and caught up with Han. "Now that's something I can understand."

"I bet you can." Han noticed the scrip. "And leave that behind. It'll be a bad end for both of us if somebody recognizes it."

"Right." Kenah dropped it on the ground as they proceeded out of the alley together. "Say, why the sudden generosity?"

"These two denarii I have seem to be burning a hole in my purse."

"Then you stole them recently?"

"Yes, yes, come on, before we're caught here."

"And you kept them hidden—"

"I told you already, so I wouldn't have to share it with the others."

"Me too?"

"Of course not. Why do you think I kept it hidden until now?"

"I don't know."

"But I just told you." Han smacked himself on the forehead with the flat of his left hand. "For heaven's sake, will you shut up?"

"But—"

"Shut up."

"But—"

"Shut . . . up!"

They proceeded along the dirty streets toward a place in the lower city where the wine was cheap and the questioning glances were rare.

Kenah stepped on something soft. "Shit!" He stopped walking and raised his right foot to inspect the bottom of his sandals.

Han chuckled. "Yeah, that's what it smells like. Serves you right."

"For what?"

"For not paying attention while making me crazy."

Han waited for him to scrape the bottom of his sandal across the edge of a single step along the street. He tried to remain patient as Kenah tried to hurry because they both secretly looked forward to getting underneath the safety of a tavern's roof—even if it was for only a little while.

CHAPTER 5

The Second Watch: Dark Inquiry and Execution

It stopped raining as the grim procession neared its destination by veering past a small cluster of herdsmen's homes—a place of outcasts in Jewish society. These predomi antly squat mud-brick dwellings were built on foundations of stone and were covered with a latticework of branches to support a roof of beaten clay. A wall had been built wherever there was a separation between two dwellings to provide some security against thieves and to ensure greater control over their own private livestock.

Ganto led the ragged column of men a considerable distance around the small settlement in order not to excite the dogs. They managed to steer past the southern end of the hamlet without incident and proceeded toward their final destination just ahead.

As soon as they reached the herdsmen's fold, Ganto posted two of his own trusted sentries to assist the cattlefold's doorkeeper, who was standing near the entrance. The doorkeeper's usual spot was at the entrance of a tiny shelter situated on a high spot nearby. But there was too much activity going on this evening, too much potential danger lurking in the darkness for the sentry to sit comfortably in his shelter. He welcomed the company of Ganto's men.

As the weary procession passed through the unlocked gate into the cattlefold's relative safety, they were greeted by a menagerie of beasts. The herdsmen had released the oxen and the asses, which were allowed to roam freely among the camels within the limits of the rectangular rock-walled perimeter of the fold. The swine had been segregated into the southeastern corner by a fence, however, and the horses had been left in their stalls at the western side of the long flat-roofed stable. Three of the four doors leading into the south side of the long stable were already closed. The fourth was about to be shut by the man in charge of the horses.

Two herdsmen, who were standing near one of the four entrances of the long stable, were rapt with anticipation. One of them stepped forward and approached Ganto immediately.

"Welcome, Ganto."

"Hello, Aher."

"Is that your man, Judas?"

"Yes."

Balak pushed Judas toward Aher. "He's the one."

The herdsman, Aher, noted that Judas's hands were not bound. "Hmm. Yet gagged, I see."

Ganto studied Aher, who continued with his preoccupation over the fact that Judas's hands were not bound.

In a world filled with scarcity, where hunger was everybody's brother and sorrow everybody's sister, where poverty made too many people thin to the bone, Ganto was always surprised by Aher's near obesity. He understood why the man was resented, even hated, for his lucrative occupation—and he knew it had nothing to do with their religious ideas concerning uncleanliness. It had to do with prosperity and envy and opportunity, as well as the willingness to accommodate pagan tastes in consuming flesh.

The man's facial features were coarse: his nose bulbous, his lips thick, his earlobes large and fleshy. Together, they seemed to make his expressions broad and as bold as his legs.

His beard needed shaping and the length of his thick black hair needed cutting. But his feet were washed and his fingernails were clean.

He was fully cloaked with a lower mantle despite the modest evening temperatures. And he always carried a staff for personal protection, although he disguised its lethal potential by pretending to depend on it for a steadier gait.

Despite his contrary physical features, his pleasing demeanor and broad sense of humor were well groomed and his generosity well beyond most men's definition of virtue.

It was Aher who dissolved the momentary tableau. "You. Convert. How did you come by your name?"

Ganto reached around and untied Judas's gag. "Answer him."

"I . . . I selected it myself," Judas said.

"You know how a convert can be," the second herds-man interjected as he stepped forward. "More Jewish than a Jew." He waited for the low-level laughter that erupted among them to subside. "Thus the name Judas signifying, to those who care, his supposed commitment as a child of Israel."

"And why not a convert?" Judas said defensively.

"With an assumed name?"

"It's legitimate. I make no secret of my chosen name and my reverence for the people I have freely chosen to bond with."

"Still sneaky if you ask me."

"I'm circumcised. I've entered Israel through this rit-ual. And I'll not explain myself any further to you," Judas said with contempt.

Ganto turned to the men in charge of Judas. "Hold him right here."

Balak pulled out his dagger and looked at Dathan as if sharing a conspiracy. "I'll take care of Judas, don't worry."

"Use that on him and I'll hang you from the nearest overhead beam inside this stable."

"But—"

"Shut up." Ganto directed his next order at two of his better men. "Watch them both." Then Ganto ambled away from Judas and toward the closed stable door, accompanied by both herdsmen to continue their discussion privately. "As you can see, this Corinthian has Galilean tendencies."

The second herdsman, Ithai, was surprised by Ganto's sympathetic remark. But Aher was amused. "There's Galilean fervor in him, that's for sure."

Ithai shrugged his shoulders. "I admit that makes the best kind of rebel."

"You better believe it," Ganto said proudly. "Even before being dispossessed from his land, a Galilean will fight for his cause."

"Then it's almost a shame you spoiled Judas by placing him among those followers of Jesus."

"I had to get somebody to do it, Ithai. And, well, he seemed the most expendable to me."

"I hope you don't think of one of us in that manner, someday."

"We're all expendable," Aher agreed.

"Thank you," Ganto said.

The corner of Ithai's mouth began to twitch. "I'm not exactly comforted by this new knowledge."

"Then you haven't been serious enough about our cause against Rome."

"That's right," Aher said. "This Judas apparently knew the risks."

"But he turned on us," Ganto said.

"I thought he merely failed to recruit those among them who followed Jesus."

"The same thing, Ithai."

"I have a problem with that."

"Then you haven't been hungry enough," Ganto said.

"Nor have you been made bitter by the loss of farmland and the death of children," Aher added in support, which pleased Ganto. "One serious look at those poor wretches standing inside our stable this very moment should be enough proof of that suffering."

Ithai shook his head. "Twisted. Everything seems so twisted."

"You can leave the cause at any time," Ganto said.

Ithai glanced at Aher, his elder, to gauge the certainty of his fate should he ever defect. "And go where? To do what? So I could eventually end up begging along the road to Jerusalem."

Aher placed one of his arms across Ithai's shoulders. "See how expendable we are?"

Ithai reluctantly nodded his head. "I only hope I'll get more sympathy if, and when, I fail."

"Don't count on it."

Ganto chuckled without cruel intent. "That's right. Don't count on anything. Failure also means Rome has got you pegged as a criminal and, once dispossessed from your property, means certain death."

Aher conveyed his sympathy by increasing the pressure of his arm against Ithai's youthful shoulders. "We're all caught in the end anyway."

"Then all I'm doing is delaying my failure and death?"

"That's right," Ganto said. "But with Rome, you have the opportunity to suffer unto death by the misfortune of crucifixion rather than by the slow death of starvation."

"Neither choice puts me at ease."

"That's good."

"Why?"

Ganto refrained from joining Aher in laughter. "It helps prevent failure. Even though Rome—"

"And Herod—"

"Always win."

Ithai seemed bewildered. "Is our cause that hopeless?"

"Yes," Ganto said. "But what else is there for a man?"

"Then . . . then Judas is a man."

"I never said he wasn't."

Aher released Ithai from his embrace. "Sooner or later a man's either caught by some kind of authority or simply gets mixed up—loses sight of the truth, whatever that is."

"But it's the same bad end in either case," Ganto said.

"Except, he dies by Rome's hand if he's caught and . . . and . . ." Ithai was unable to finish his line of thought.

Aher glanced past Ithai at Ganto. "And dies by our hand if it's the other."

Ganto saw Ithai's eyes widen. "Steady, my young friend. It's a desperate night and there are many low-spirited men in that stable in need of an entertaining diversion to go along with their meager handfuls of corn."

"Morale is very low among our men," Aher confirmed.

"It seems that we are no better than these Romans and their circuses," Ithai declared.

"That's true," Ganto said firmly.

"Then . . . then is that fair?" Ithai persisted.

"To whom?"

"To Judas, of course."

"What's fair?" Ganto grinned sinisterly. "Don't worry. We will be just and merciful."

"That's right," Aher added. "You must always remember: the thrust from one of our daggers is quick and clean, while the snap of the hangman's noose is humane and deadly. In either case, these are better deaths than any Roman execution. Whatever the pain, it's not overly prolonged."

"Somehow, that seems small comfort to me, right now," Ithai said.

"Don't worry, it's later, much later, when you'll see the greater comfort." Ganto finally turned from them, displaying his growing impatience. "Let's take Judas inside where it's safer."

"Through that door," Ithai said. "This stable is large enough to accommodate many of us."

"That's right," said Aher. "And as you instructed, I had the word passed among those who would be interested."

"Good," said Ganto.

"In fact, there are already quite a few men inside waiting with great interest."

"But I suspect," Ithai interjected, "that for many of those inside, it's the only interest in town."

"You mean, their only shelter tonight," Ganto said.

"That's right," said Aher. "A night's lodging is the best I can do. That and a bit of milk and a handful of parched corn—"

"And Judas. Don't forget my Judas. It's a circus, remember?" Ganto declared. "And his performance will soften their misery."

"But what class of merriment is this?" Ithai challenged, rankled by Ganto's callousness.

"Dark merriment. Very, very dark." Ganto was beginning to lose his patience with Ithai. He turned to Aher. "I'll pay you for your losses," Ganto declared, "from the goods I manage to take on my next raid against a Roman baggage train, I promise."

"I'm not worried."

"Thank you, brother. Lead the way."

But a disturbance within the cattlefold caught their attention:

"Look out!"

"Get him!"

"A dagger, watch out!"

Ganto rushed over to the scene and discovered Judas backing toward the fold's exit with a dagger in his hand. Judas's threatening posture was made more ominous by the numerous shadow-causing oil lamps that were held by the men that surrounded him. "Where did he get that weapon!"

"I don't know," Balak said with great distress. "The son of a bitch pushed me—and there it was!"

Judas slashed at several men who tried to disarm him. "Get back. I don't want to hurt anybody."

"Give it up, Judas," said Ganto. "You know it's hopeless."

"Then you know I've nothing to lose."

Two of Ganto's men unsuccessfully attacked Judas from the side.

"Careful with him," Ganto cautioned. "He's too desperate to disarm."

Judas reached the cattlefold's gate and opened it. "I'll kill the next man who tries to get near me."

As soon as Judas backed through the gate, Ganto's sentries assaulted him. The blow to the back of his head with a smooth bulbous rod stunned Judas long enough for them to grab both his arms, dislodge the dagger from his hand, and pin him in an upright position between them. Then they escorted him, with his feet dragging, back into the cattlefold.

Ganto's anger increased with each statement. "Good work. Bind his hands. And search him, damn it!"

Balak held the point of his dagger against Judas's throat. "See what you get when you treat a man like a human being?"

"Balak's right," said Dathan.

"Enough already," Ganto exploded. "I'll not be like a Roman." He peered at Aher, a little disoriented by his anger. "Let's go."

"This way," Aher quickly said in an effort to help neutralize Ganto's mood.

They escorted Judas into the stable, where they were greeted by a mob consisting of peasants and beggars and destitute men, a mob fortified by the relatively well-fed warriors of Ganto's robber band.

"What happened, Ganto?" asked a nameless peasant without teeth. "We heard noise outside."

Ganto was so dismayed by the number of men present, that he didn't hear the beggar. So, Balak answered him instead. "This lout tried to escape."

Forced to stare at the man because of close proximity, Judas could've sworn the beggar had leprosy. He'd seen enough of this affliction while he and his brethren traveled the highway with their Master. Yet, nobody in the stable seemed alarmed by this man's presence among them.

Aher nudged Ganto's arm. "As you can see, I've set up a raised platform near the center of the stable for you."

"Excellent, Aher. Excellent."

"Through these men is the only way to the platform." Aher began pushing for the way ahead. "Come on."

Aher, Judas, Ganto and the others pushed through the tightly-packed crowd comprised of desperate men filled with anticipation. Many, dressed in rags, were still nursing their handful of parched corn: to eat quickly, to swallow without slow and thoughtful chewing after long periods of hunger, was a waste. Their emaciated skulls made the wide-open expressions in their eyes appear more bizarre, almost childlike.

"Balak, you old sawhorse. Is that you?"

"Jakim, you scoundrel!" Balak broke away from Judas, confident that it was impossible for him to attempt another escape.

"These herdsmen have been generous. Is your stomach empty?"

"When isn't it?" Balak retorted, as he joined Jakim and disappeared within the throng of men.

When Dathan saw that Balak had begun to improve his material condition, he quickly sought to do the same. He peeled away from Ganto and his men and disappeared into the crowd in search for a possible handful of parched corn.

None of this escaped Ganto's attention, who remained sympathetic toward both these hungry men.

When they reached the edge of the platform, Igeal, one of Ganto's newer followers, who had helped construct this circus arena, stepped forward. "Say, I recognize him. Wasn't that you who stepped in front of Jesus when I approached him with my dagger?"

"It was," Judas said defiantly.

"A quick assassination was the plan."

"I couldn't," said Judas.

"Nice. Now that poor bastard's suffering a miserable death because of you, right Huri?"

"Yeah," Huri agreed as he wiped a few drops of milk off his beard with the back of his filthy forearm. "They say everybody wanted him out of the way. He was a rebel to Rome, a troublemaker to Herod, and a neutralizer to the people both for and against violence."

"He was too smart for his own good," Igeal said.

"That's true," said Huri. "He possessed too much vision with too little time at hand. But there was no question he was a patriot and a true child of Israel. Rome was going to crucify him no matter what. That—that was inevitable. All we could have done was save this Jesus from his torture. Hell, he's no criminal to have been mistreated like that. He should have, could have died swiftly, painlessly, and with dignity like so many of us have cried out for when faced with Rome's execution. We could have given him a good death. But you saved him for a bad death."

"It wasn't my fault," Judas said defensively. "I didn't mean it. I . . . I didn't know."

Huri slapped Igeal on the back with dismay. "That's common knowledge among us, stupid."

Igeal chuckled. "And that's why you're still alive—"

"And quivering with guilt. Guilt! It's your fault he's hanging on the wood, gentile convert! Yours and yours alone."

Ganto finally stepped between Judas and these two men. "Easy men, easy. We haven't even started his inquiry yet and we're calling him names."

"What inquiry?" Judas demanded.

"Why, this one. Lift him up to the platform," Ganto commanded.

Without waiting for Ganto to repeat himself, some of the men grabbed Judas, lifted him into the air, and set him on the platform, which stood about waist level to the crowd by resting on a foundation of sawhorses. Judas instinctively shuffled toward the center of it to keep himself out of reach from the standing crowd that pressed against its four edges.

Judas looked out among the men and wondered why there was so much hatred directed toward him. None of these men knew him except for those in Ganto's band, or the few he'd seen in the streets of Jerusalem, or those he'd seen listening to his Master in the countryside. Upon second thought, he did know a significant number of these men. Then he noticed one in particular whose name escaped his memory—wait!—Joses. It was Joses! But what in the world was he doing here?

The din of activity—eating and drinking, pushing and shoving—as well as the constant murmur of obscenities punctuated by laughter, made it difficult for Judas to think. But he made the effort to recollect: Joses was a righteous man among the followers of his Master—a brethren.

Judas tried to make eye contact with Joses, but it was hopeless. There was too much activity in the stable for any kind of private exchange.

Harsh plosive laughter drew Judas's attention away from Joses toward a small clique of men who were being entertained by a dwarf. Satisfied with the results of his antics, the dwarf snatched a small cup out of another man's hand, dipped it into a large milk jar, then brought it to his lips. He tilted the cup so steeply as he drank, that much of the milk ran down the front of his filthy sackcloth tunic. It was an extravagant act for a destitute man.

Judas averted his eyes from the dwarf and looked across the panorama of men before him. Because of the numerous flickering handheld oil lamps and lanterns, shadows danced and streaked along every surface: the walls, the overhead, and the floor. Also, the constant movement of these men packed into this enclosure increased the drama of the shadow play several more times. Judas began to tremble at the sight. It was a scene that writhed like a tangled multitude of snakes in a pit at his feet. The stench of uncleanliness suddenly assaulted him with the scent of desperate men and skittish beasts. He almost panicked.

In one long and steady movement, he turned and looked in all four directions and saw that he was completely surrounded. Then he looked up and saw a center beam supporting a latticework of branches that made the flat roof of the structure. He wished he could see the sky. He wished, Lord he wished he could be elsewhere. He didn't have any idea what Ganto had in mind to do to him or what it was, exactly, Ganto had against him outside of the thirty pieces of silver and his failure to recruit Jesus and his inability to be an assassin—my God. But the silver could have been easily explained. Easily proved! And why all of this . . . this—

"This is a mockery!" Judas shouted as he looked down at Ganto.

"Shut up!" Ganto countered. The men near Ganto jostled each other to give him plenty of space. "And quiet down, everybody. Quiet down, I say!"

Silence rippled throughout the crowd of men until there was nothing left but a low restless murmur. The men anxiously pressed against each other to keep out of Ganto's way.

Ganto walked in a tight arc until he completed a circle, then stopped. "There's a strange feeling in the air this dark hour. One of revolt and, yet, nobody seems to want to take up arms. There's anger but no fight, resentment but no action. People seem to be loitering uneasily here and there and into the night—some with and some without the comfort of a lamp. What is it, I wonder?"

"Could it be this Jesus?" Dathan suggested from within the safety of the crowd.

Ganto grimaced. "Nah. He's just another executed peasant."

"You really think so?"

Ganto hesitated. "I don't know."

"There are many women grieving over his crucifixion."

"Yes, I heard. But why?"

"They say he acted as if he were the Messiah."

"Bah, he's a seller of snake oil," said Ganto.

"But Dathan's right," Balak insisted. "I've heard there are those who believe he *is* the Messiah."

"And everything does seem to be at a standstill," Dathan said. "I'm like you, Ganto. I don't understand all this tendency for nonviolent revolt by ordinary people such as ourselves."

"Ordinary!" Ganto laughed. "You're much too generous in describing a crowd of peasants, beggars, and thieves." Ganto looked at Judas. "Alright. You're supposed to know more about this man than any of us."

Judas searched as many pairs of eyes that allowed him to do so. "What do I know?"

"You've spent lots of time with him," Ganto said. "You've got to know something worth telling. Something—fundamental."

"Go on Judas," Balak said with disdain. "Try and save yourself."

"That's right," Ganto said. "Save yourself, Judas."

Judas stood helplessly silent for a long while, knowing that any attempt to explain Jesus' love and peace to them was hopeless. Even the people who heard Jesus themselves—himself, for example, didn't fully understand his words.

"Well?" Ganto said. "We're waiting. Was this man a sage or a lunatic?"

Judas nervously wiped the sweat off his brow with the back of his forearm. "I don't know."

"Was he a warrior or a scribe?"

"He spoke like a scribe, Ganto!" shouted one of the nameless men. Then several different men in the crowd expressed their anxieties by projecting a cavalcade of remarks:

"He never spoke against Rome."

"Then why must Rome be so brutal to us?"

"Yeah."

"Herod's no different!"

"Imagine—Herod worse to us than Pilate."

"The Idumean bastard!"

"Alright, quiet down, everybody," Ganto said. "Let Judas speak—"

"If he can!"

"I said quiet!" Ganto turned to Judas. "I understand these men. But I neither understand you nor the source of those other strange ideas floating about." Ganto studied Judas momentarily. "I believe you have truly fallen under the influence of this man, leaving you at a standstill with contradictions and a strange new sense of guilt that I don't comprehend."

"You put me there," Judas said accusingly.

Ganto's anger flared. "But you chose to stay until you caught its leprosy rather than fleeing from them and reporting to me."

"And what could I have said that would have made sense to you?"

"Don't play words with me, Judas. There was nothing to say, but the truth."

"The truth! The truth?" Judas approached the edge of the platform. "What is the truth?"

"I don't know. It's . . . it's something between the words, something in the look in one's eye. I know it when I see it; I'm aware of it when I hear it."

"From . . . from an understanding found between two words? You can do better than that," Judas said.

Ganto knitted his brow with uncertainty. "And from something in your eyes."

"And?"

"And . . . and we'll see where the truth comes from by a court of seventeen selected from among these men." Ganto turned to the crowd. "To those I point to, stand over there." Then he randomly selected men he did not personally know. As soon as Ganto was satisfied with the ragged group that now stood apart from the rest, he turned to Judas. "There you are: our smaller version of the Sanhedrin."

"With you as the high priest?"

Ganto's uninspired laughter drew silence among those in the crowd. "Now speak, Judas. Speak the words of this so-called messiah. Speak his version of truth or I'll not be able to save you. Convince these select men—convince me, the high priest."

Of what? Judas desperately thought. The silence before him sent a chill down his back. He needed a drink. God, he could use a drink.

Judas stood quietly for a few moments before he raised his bound hands in front of him to help express himself. "Jesus. Jesus was often not a sober prophet, if you ask me. Still, I heard him speak on many occasions and I almost became a true follower. But just enough wine *and* a fair share of women, kept me satisfied often enough to prevent me from deserting him and his disciples." The laughter that followed Judas's strained humor, encouraged him to go on. "But let's face it, he's been executed as a political agitator and a criminal, which he simply was in Pilate's eyes—the clever evil bastard. He knew that Jesus was a real messenger of revolution among the people. If Jesus hadn't been so cunning by dressing his rebellion in statements such as 'love your enemies' and 'turn the other cheek,' he would have been nailed onto a crossbeam by these Romans long before now." Judas's voice suddenly dropped to a whisper. "The truth of the matter is, and Jesus stated this many times to the crowd, that 'he came not to bring peace, but a sword.' " Judas noticed the strained expressions among those further away from the platform. "He even threatened to destroy the Temple! Believe me, that made our own corrupt Jewish officials afraid of him. They even considered him mad." He slowly walked along the edge of the platform until he reached the point where he started. "The closest understanding I ever came to an idea of his was this: his Kingdom of God was right here in Palestine without Rome's presence. God and the land and our heritage were all one. This Nazarene was no fool—he was a visionary who made fools of us all by our own lack of understanding."

"But what made this Nazarene a great man in your eyes?" Ganto asked. "A prophet even."

Judas licked his dry lips. "Even though I'm nothing, I'll tell you. He blessed the poor. He blessed those who were hungered. And he blessed me—made me feel like a man of some worth."

"But we live in violent times!" Huri shouted. Ganto stepped aside, then positioned himself opposite the mock Sanhedrin court to indicate that it was alright for anybody to address Judas at this time. "I said we live in violent times!"

Judas looked directly at Huri. "And Jesus was not afraid to confront that violence—even provoke it." Judas shook his head. "I don't know." He raised his bound hands to his mouth and rubbed the crusts of dryness from its corners. "He was a clever troublemaker. And, in a way, I liked that. He made our priests and scribes look stupid and avoided Pilate's might for almost three years. Somehow . . . somehow he transcended violence while he stirred the people against Herod's injustice and Rome's brutality. He made me proud to be a Jew."

Judas's last statement caused many to grumble.

"And what about this kingdom he spoke about?" Huri pressed. "You said it was right here in Palestine." Huri mimicked looking around as if searching for something. "I don't see anything."

Judas shrugged his shoulders. "All I can say, well, I'll just say his words about the Kingdom somehow brought me face to face with eternity."

"That won't fill an empty belly!" Dathan declared.

The men restlessly shifted and stirred about while they murmured in agreement.

"But it might fill an empty soul," Judas said.

This remark further agitated the crowd.

"You speak as if you understood this man," Balak taunted. "Even trusted him."

"If you'd . . . you'd lived with him, perhaps . . . perhaps you'd have better understood him."

"Or misunderstood him," said Balak. "But you still haven't answered Huri. You still haven't explained this kingdom Jesus spoke about with your word, eternity."

Judas placed his bound hands against the back of his head in an effort to physically support his internal search. "The Kingdom of God . . . the Kingdom of God . . . is about God's rule."

"That's right, more double talk!" one of the nameless men shouted.

"No! What I mean . . . what he sometimes meant, I think—God's Kingdom is in our very midst at last! It is present, with us and not only in heaven, to finally help liberate us. At least . . . at least, sometimes—I think."

"Does that mean God will finally provide us with weapons?" Huri said facetiously.

Cruel laughter erupted from all corners of the stable.

"Even I know God does not work in that way," Judas said impatiently.

"Then how?" somebody shouted angrily, as somebody else from the side nearest the stalled horses threw a piece of dung at Judas—it hit him in the chest.

Ganto leaped onto the platform beside Judas in response. "Enough of that! I'll not have anymore of that!" The men grew somber over Ganto's rebuke, knowing he was capable of carrying out his threat. And as soon as Ganto was sure that he was fully understood, he looked at Judas. "Go on."

Judas was shaken by the growing animosity toward him. But Ganto's decision to remain on the platform made him feel better. "I believe ... I believe it will be through us that God will satisfy our desire for prosperity."

A poor, middle-aged Pharisee finally broke his silence and wound his way through the crowd toward the edge of the platform. He was a coppersmith by necessity and a scholar by choice, who wore a plain tunic made of linen that was tied to the waist with a belt. The lightweight mantle that was wrapped across his chest was kept in place by draping it over his left shoulder. His full beard was carefully trimmed. And just below the lower edge of his white turban, a pair of sharp eyes glistened.

"Right now I'd be thankful for just laws and plain order," the Pharisee declared.

There was a general murmur of agreement among the other men.

"Good one there, Rabbi," said one of the nameless ones among the crowd.

"And don't forget a full belly!" Dathan added.

"Shut up, Dathan. That's all you ever care about." Igeal peered at the Pharisee. "A man needs more than that in the long run."

Dathan pushed past the men in front of him and took several threatening steps towards Igeal. "Yeah? Try running long without one."

Both men squared off prepared to fight.

Judas stooped toward them from the platform. "Men, please—we're not supposed to fight among ourselves. That's the very thing he was talking about."

"Who?" Dathan snapped. "Oh, you mean, Jesus."

"Loving your enemy, Igeal, and turning your cheek, Dathan, is supposed to give us patience and unity against Rome."

"I'll not let a Roman soldier slap me," Dathan said.

"And I don't blame you," Judas said, taking advantage of the momentary respite from their hostility. "He's another kind of enemy."

"A true enemy."

"That's right."

Dathan countered Judas with a satire. "Oh, I see. I see." He turned to Igeal and placed his right hand on Igeal's shoulder. "I'm sorry for my anger." This drew a round of laughter throughout the stable.

Igeal placed his hand on top of Dathan's. "And I'm sorry for my sharp tongue."

"Well, that's quite an amusing performance," said the Pharisee. "But Rome is still very much with us and I don't foresee it being otherwise for a very long time."

"I don't really think Jesus meant to make changes by tomorrow, Rabbi. Even beyond the tomorrow of our lives." Judas noted that this wasn't what they wanted to hear. "But I think he meant to give us something to do; meant to give us hope."

"I'll not argue that point," the rabbi said.

The stable full of men began to grow quiet with interest, as well as with respect for the rabbi's active involvement. This alerted Judas. In fact, the sudden and relative silence heightened his anxiety.

"But you speak with too many contradictions, Judas," the rabbi added. "First you said God's Kingdom is in our midst, then it's in heaven."

"He said, Rabbi, he said!" Judas's eyes bulged with denial.

"You also say he's a revolutionary—but only for tomorrow."

"Not a sober prophet, remember?"

"I see. One who also says 'turn the other cheek,' but be sure to bring a sword."

"What . . . what can I . . . I say?" Judas stammered. "He firmly spoke, spoke of love and compassion."

"But so does any rabbi."

"He spoke of wisdom and . . . and restraint."

"As would any rabbi."

Judas inhaled deeply, then forcefully blurted his next phrase without pause. "You are to love the Lord with all your heart *and* are to love your neighbor as yourself!"

"Then that made Jesus a pious Jew since he loved God and his fellow man."

"But—"

"And to love your neighbor as yourself is," the rabbi continued, "well, the Torah speaks of this as a comprehensive precept. In fact, the Torah speaks of love as a moral necessity and urges us not to hate our enemy or seek vengeance. And further still, our sacred scripture urges us to help and pray and even befriend our enemies. So. What kind of good news did this man teach that isn't already taught in the synagogue?"

"But to turn the cheek—"

"Are simply new words—not a new idea."

Judas pressed his bound hands against his chin. "Then . . . then what was his point?"

"His point? His point, I think, was clear."

"Then enlighten me, please," Judas said with a tone of defiance in his voice.

The rabbi thoughtfully rubbed his lower lip with his left forefinger; the sound of breathing could be heard throughout the stable. "This man—I know he often spoke of the Kingdom of God."

"He did," Judas retorted.

"But where is this Kingdom, again?"

"Well it's . . . it's at hand. It's, well—you tell me."

The rabbi shrugged his shoulders and directed his next statement to some of the nearby men. "Perhaps it is at hand. Perhaps." An intense murmur spread throughout the attentive crowd. "But according to what I've heard about your teacher, it's *mostly* in heaven."

"That's right," Judas enthusiastically said. "We're to enter the Kingdom of God *in heaven*."

"Yes. In heaven." The rabbi took a couple of backward steps from the edge of the platform. The men standing behind him quickly maneuvered out of his way like a parting sea. "Instead of establishing the Kingdom of God on earth, you must enter heaven. And that is the basic difference between me and that man. Your prophet despairs of human nature; he rejects this world instead of embracing it. But I say we are not only spirit—we are human as well; human. We are of the earth! And by man's righteous efforts—with His divine help—we will enter the Kingdom of God right here on earth someday."

"Good one, Rabbi," an unidentified man standing close by uttered.

"But you . . . you don't understand!" Judas shouted. "You had to be there!"

The rabbi waited for both Judas and the surrounding men to calm down. "And what? Temporarily fall under the spell of his charisma and contradictions?"

Judas paced toward several edges of the platform like a caged animal. "Alright. Alright! I know I'm the limited one and do injustice to his message. But why do you attack him so?"

"I've never called *him* a viper or a sepulcher," the rabbi countered. "True, there are some among us who act immorally and others who are inflexible about Temple worship. But we are human and, therefore, are not without sin *and* are not without the ordinary need for repentance and atonement." He shrugged his shoulders and addressed several ragged men nearby. "I'm not offering attacks—only questions. I'm only seeking to comprehend." He turned his attention back to Judas. "And from what I understand, your teacher has offered us nothing new except … except for what is not *in* this world. His kingdom is ultimately not of this world."

"If you say so, Rabbi," one of the ragged men said as the others enthusiastically jostled each other like children.

"There are others who believe this to be true," Judas declared.

The rabbi continued to address the ragged men. "Yes. Disheartened brethren who are looking toward the supernatural for escape. Yes. We've become a desperate people. But still, we are not without vigorous hope, sober faith, realistic traditions, and trust in our land, our blood, our God."

Judas stomped on the platform with his right foot to get the rabbi's attention. "Then to you, he's just another failed messiah."

"Those are Ganto's words. Right Ganto?"

"I don't care about religion, Rabbi. I care about oppression and injustice when I speak."

The rabbi humbly bowed his head to acknowledge Ganto's firm statement.

"But wait," Judas insisted. "You don't understand. To have been near this man was to become intoxicated with him."

"Be careful." The rabbi approached the platform on the edge of anger. "This kind of intoxication comes close to worship."

Judas stepped toward him, knelt on one knee, and lowered his head to gain more intimacy with the rabbi. "No less intoxicating than your worship for scrolls."

The rabbi maintained his composure, determined not to be intimidated by Judas's desperation. "The study of the sacred scrolls is a form of worship, yes. But it's not the worship *of* a physical thing."

The side of Judas's mouth twitched with discomfort. "I admit I sometimes revered this man and his preaching."

"And what about what's written?"

Judas shrugged his shoulders. "Is written."

"Your statement of finality only shows your ignorance," the rabbi said heatedly.

"Jesus didn't write. He spoke of change," Judas said defiantly. "And there are many who believe him."

"But change grows from our writing about belief and practice."

Judas shook his head. "No. There's too much writing. Too much Law—like Ganto said. You spit into the wind."

"Don't confuse 'too much' with adjustments and reformulations of our Laws."

"Oh, that's very clever, Rabbi. Do anything to make the Law palatable to the common man. The weight of our Law still strangles a man, right Ganto?"

To everybody's growing surprise, Ganto remained silent.

The rabbi pressed his face closer to Judas's. "And having no Law invites danger and turmoil within the heart and across our land."

"Scholar."

"I choose to ignore the curse in your tone, Judas, and accept that word as a blessing."

Judas stood up and addressed the mob. "See how clever these Pharisees are? See how they use words?"

"You can't have it both ways," said the rabbi. "In the end, you have to choose your beliefs."

"But I've ... I've already admitted to all of you that I don't fully understand Jesus."

"Or yourself, it seems," the Pharisee said, as he backed away from Judas and joined the surrounding men.

Judas looked at Igeal, then at Dathan with mounting confusion. "It's my confidence. It waxes and wanes constantly when I'm left on my own."

"Especially when you drink too much!" Huri shouted.

Laughter exploded throughout the stable.

"Boy, that's obvious!" a nameless one added.

The Pharisee waited for some of the raucousness to subside. "Then what good is any of your understanding?"

"If you had sat at that man's banquet table one time, you would have discovered my . . . my confused dilemma for yourself," Judas said firmly.

The Pharisee squinted his eyes and wrinkled his nose. "But I'm already confused. Why would I want more of it to eat?"

"Well said, Rabbi," somebody cheered. "Well said."

"Hell," Dathan cracked, "even I'd get drunk with that fellow if he made sense."

The stable full of men broke out in laughter and back-slapping again.

"Who are you kidding, Dathan! You're a whore," Igeal shouted. "You'd eat and drink with a demon if it were free."

Dathan blushed as the laughter turned against him. "Bite my ass."

Ganto finally took control of the situation again. "Alright, Dathan, move along. I think we've heard enough about your needs." And as the laughter increased, Ganto looked at Huri and pointed to the rafter above Judas.

Huri was anticipating Ganto's command—the coiled rope was already in his hand. He flaked out the tail end of it, tossed the rope over the beam, and pulled on its running length until the noose on the other end was level with Judas's head.

Judas trembled at its sight. "What is this!"

"It's clear that this prophet didn't oppose violence," Ganto said, ignoring Judas. "But he managed somehow to keep it at a distance. And for that, I don't trust the man."

"But—"

"I didn't say I didn't like him, Judas. Or that he wasn't truly one of us. But I simply don't trust something I don't fully understand."

"But—"

"You've had your say. This so-called messiah was no triumphant leader. How was he going to throw off the yoke of our oppression and restore Israel by dying? It's obvious he was a fake. God didn't arm him with any power to lead and rule our people. Where's the prosperity in his crucifixion? Where's our freedom—our peace? He was false— false, I say!" He pressed the flat of his hand against his chest. "Believe me by seeing for yourself that I speak the obvious truth." Ganto looked at Judas with an evil grin that turned mischievous when he looked down at Huri. "Hang him."

"No, Ganto!" the Pharisee cried. "You can't! What about your Sanhedrin court?"

"Don't play moral games with *me*, Rabbi. I'm the law here in this den of peasants and thieves and cutthroats! I'm Caesar of this underworld of nobodies! In here you're nothing, do you understand me, nothing!"

In response to Ganto's ferocity, the Pharisee calmly withdrew into the crowd; the surrounding men grew silent and still and expectant while another man weaved through the mob to reach the opposite side of the platform where he climbed onboard, stepped alongside Judas, and placed his right arm across Judas's trembling shoulders. The man drew everybody's attention away from the Pharisee by this unexpected conduct. Ganto was bewildered when he finally turned around to see what was going on, and then he became curious—he found this man's demeanor strange, even unsettling.

"My name is Joses," said the man.

Ganto deliberately went to the other end of the platform and openly studied the man.

Joses was dark and serious, poor but clean. He did not carry himself like a laborer, but anyone could see he was no stranger to hardship. His knee-length tunic was plain and was gathered at the waist with a strand of coarse rope. The man's long black hair was almost straight and his head was as bare as his feet.

By directing a single nod at this unexpected participant, Ganto confirmed the man's right to be there as well as invited him to continue speaking. "Okay, Joses." He jumped off the stage and looked up at him. "Speak."

"We are nothing but misfits," said Joses.

"With a cause," Ganto firmly qualified.

Joses glanced at Judas as if he were seeking his support. "But now I think we're beginning to act like criminals."

"Oh, do you now? Imagine that." Ganto drew laughter from the crowd. "But the villagers love us, even harbor us."

"True," Joses said, "and they'll go on dying to protect us."

"Us? I'm not sure about us," Ganto said suspiciously.

"Yeah, who is that guy?" somebody shouted.

"I've never seen him before," said another.

"There's our spy!"

Ganto raised his hands to calm the men before their concern started to get out of control. "Alright, alright." But Ganto didn't like the implication of Joses' last statement either. "I can't help their death. And I won't feel guilty." Ganto took a threatening step toward Joses, who steered Judas between them. Then Ganto turned away from the pair and looked out among the men. "It's a desperate circumstance for those of us who've been driven off our land!"

"And for those who are on the verge of the same!" somebody squawked hysterically.

"Yeah!"

"I'm no different!" Joses proudly yelled. He released Judas from his embrace in a fit of anger. "I'm sick to death of Roman terror!—of Roman reprisals!—of Rome's massive violence against us! It's making me crazy!"

The effect of Ganto's laughter in response was like a splash of water on Joses' face. "Careful, Joses. Or you'll end up possessed."

"I'll not let demons occupy me. I don't care what Rome does to me."

Joses' last statement caused a series of outcries:

"The whip will make you care alright!"

"Yeah! Brave talk for one so young!"

"Rome knows how to strike terror in my heart!"

"Yeah! I was once possessed!"

Ganto raised his hands and, like a conductor, gestured for reduced intensity. Then he saw one of the nameless ones pick up a piece of dung. He pointed directly at the man. "Throw that and you'll dance at the end of this noose!" A hush filled the stable as the man hesitated, forcing the intensity of these men to turn inward. "Drop it, I say." The man dropped the dung and wiped his hand across his chest in a display of innocence, which caused a few nervous chuckles to ripple among the spectators and defuse much of the tension. With control restored, Ganto directed his attention back to Joses. "I heard that our latest crucified prophet had the ability to drive out demons."

"Yes."

"So what," Ganto said. "It's pointless to be free of demons, but not free of Rome. If they were so weak to be possessed once, they'll be possessed again. Besides, once these people are free, where are they going to go? They went to demons because they lost everything and they'll go back to them when the weight of that reality fully bears down upon them again."

"You're a hard man, Ganto."

"I'm a realist, Joses. And these are hard times. Now step down."

Joses hesitated. But two of Ganto's very reliable men stepped up beside Judas and crowded Joses off the platform without having to threaten him with actual violence. Then one of them grabbed the noose and brought it toward Judas, who backed away into the firm arms of the other man.

"But wait. Wait!" Judas shrieked.

The man threw the noose over his neck and cinched it tightly.

"Agh. I'm innocent! Innocent."

Then the man tied his feet together. Judas was too frightened to give them any resistance.

"I'm innocent!" Judas yammered.

Ganto waited until the other man released his hold on Judas. "Innocent of what?"

Judas was delirious with confusion. "Of . . . of whatever you think me wrong!"

One of the outside sentries burst into the stable. "Quick!" he shouted as the door slammed shut behind him. "Cover your lamps! A Roman detachment is approaching!"

"Gag Judas," Ganto ordered.

One of Ganto's men on the platform quickly removed Judas's noose and then pushed him off the platform into the outstretched arms of several men waiting below, who gagged and pinned him to the ground. Everybody else scurried toward silence and darkness—the legionnaires could be heard marching by the cattlefold on the road leading toward Golgotha.

Ganto, Aher, and Huri managed to push their way to one of the stable doors and huddle against it.

"What do you suppose they're doing?" Huri whispered through the darkness.

"Must be a change of guard," Ganto stated flatly, while trying to catch a glimpse of something through the crack between the double doors.

"Or an increase in security," Aher muttered. "There's much unrest tonight."

"Yeah," Huri added nervously. "Bad weather. Executions. Passover restlessness. Hordes of disgruntled pilgrims. Conditions seem right for a riot."

"And these Romans are no fools," Aher quickly added, infected by Huri's apprehension.

"Easy you two," Ganto grumbled. "Bah, I can't see a thing." Then Ganto stiffened suddenly; the noise of speculation had intensified throughout the stable to an alarming level. He turned away from the stable's door and peered toward the hovered men blanketed by the darkness. "Keep it down," Ganto hailed as loud as he dared. "All of you! Aher: come with me. Huri: keep them under control."

The two of them eased past the partially opened door of the stable to go see what was happening for themselves.

The tense crowd of men that was left behind with Huri listened to the lumbering Roman detachment. They seemed to be taking their time and, at one point, seemed to have come to a halt. After a while, random whispers pierced the darkness, which quickly grew into a vehement undertone of strained voices:

"Those bastards. I can kill them all."

"Shhh! Quiet," said Huri.

"I've been under one kind of foreign rule or another all my life and I'm sick of it."

"Me too. I say we fight."

"Shhh!"

"But I don't have a weapon."

"Then kill a legionnaire and steal his sword."

"Yeah!" another added. "And I'll not pay any more tribute!"

"You haven't paid any in years. They robbed you of everything you had a long time ago."

A cascade of suppressed chuckles and giggles followed.

"Shhh, damn you!" Huri said.

"I speak as the man I was."

"Forget him. He perished under the weight of debt long ago."

Humor gave way to discontent and grumbling throughout the stable, leaving Huri exasperated. "Shhh! You'll have those legionnaires down on us with all this grumbling." But they continued to ignore him while pouring out hatred:

"You know the rule—payment without fail. To Rome, nonpayment is the same as rebellion."

"And the rich are no different about their loans."

"That's true. One of those bastards took my land, then paid me starvation wages for my labor."

"Shhh!"

"And our women and children suffer terribly."

"Especially! My family perished through hunger. And who was there to help? No one!"

"Steady. You have us now."

"I don't care about us. I cared about them. Where was Israel for them? Where was God?"

"Shhh."

"There's no point going into all of that."

"It's why we're here, isn't it? Well, isn't it?"

"This is an inquiry against one of us—not God."

A rush of fresh air entered the stable with the abrupt opening of the door—Ganto had returned with Aher from their reconnaissance.

Ganto waited until the stable door was closed before he spoke. "It's a good thing that detachment was a good distance away." He squinted at Huri, fuming with anger. "I thought I told you to keep them under control."

"I tried. But these fools wouldn't listen to—"

"I don't want excuses!" Ganto turned toward the crowded darkness. "You damn idiots! You sound like a bunch of festival clowns in here." Ganto had the nearest man uncover his lamp; it threw out more shadow than light. "What is it among you that would allow bitterness and discontent to prevail over good sense? What? Those legionnaires would have slaughtered us."

The flickering of other lamps began to randomly appear here and there, revealing partial features in this faceless crowd.

"Not too many lamps," Ganto ordered. "Don't uncover any more lamps, yet. Aher."

"Yes."

"Let me know when more light is safe."

"Right."

As soon as Aher left the stable, the dark faceless crowd addressed Ganto:

"I say we go into Jerusalem and riot," said one of the nameless ones.

"Yeah. With Passover in progress, the time is perfect."

"He's right," ventured one more. "People are still streaming in from the countryside to participate in the festival. It's a fitting time—"

"For a blood bath! Not a riot," Ganto said coldly, his arms akimbo and his eyes smoldering like a pair of hot coals. By the tone in Ganto's voice, nobody dared to respond. "You idiots. Do you think Pilate isn't aware of this? Especially today? Everywhere you look his legionnaires are present—not to mention Herod's Temple police. They're waiting—aching for a mass protest by these added pilgrims."

"But rioting is all we have left to express our needs."

"But at what price?" Ganto said as he waded in among them. "Too much of our own blood runs from a short sword's blade, already."

A broken man placed a weak hand on Ganto's shoulder. "The price of bread is too high. And there are too many of us sleeping in the streets—respectable working men, not just criminals and vagrants and misfits. They—we must be helped." A sympathetic murmur undulated across the tightly packed sea of men.

Ganto floated steadily among them to prevent himself from drowning. "Grumble all you want. But nobody listens to dogs, believe me."

"But we're people! Good people," a man hollered from behind.

Ganto began swimming to maintain his head above the surface of these damaged souls. "We are poor. And therefore, in their eyes, we are bad—no—we *are* dogs."

Several men grunted as others snarled in response.

"We can gather together and try to speak to them," an uncertain but rational voice suggested.

"We'll still be attacked." Ganto planted himself where he stood. "It's the official way, you know that. How many of us must be slaughtered in the streets for you to be convinced?"

"Our people have been successful with Pilate before," someone whined.

Ganto realized he was standing beside the platform. He climbed up on it and stood at the center of their uncertainty. "You mean when Tiberius first sent him here as governor of Judea?"

"Yes! He brought Caesar's standards into Jerusalem, causing wild protest from our people—both town and country folk."

Ganto recognized the voice and peered into its direction. "Ah, it's you again, Joses." Despite his earlier command, a few more lamps had been gradually uncovered, revealing distinct faces from within the faceless crowd at his feet—one in particular, Joses. "We all know the story."

Joses nervously approached the edge of the platform, closer to Ganto's scrutiny. "Our people surrounded Pilate's residence and fell prostrate for five whole days. Then on the sixth day he had his legionnaires surround them and threatened to cut them down if they continued to reject Caesar's image. He even signaled his troops to draw their swords. But our people were prepared to die rather than transgress the Law. They say that Pilate was actually frightened by this kind of devotion and had the standards removed."

Ganto looked up at the overhead and forcefully exhaled to display impatience instead of a weary sigh. "Proving what?"

"That we can make a difference if we keep a cool head," said Joses.

"That was an exception," Ganto pointed out. "Pilate was new to our world." Ganto grew somber. "He hasn't made that mistake again."

"Nor bent to our will no matter how carefully presented," Huri added.

"That's what I said," Ganto blurted irritably. "He'll beat any mob with cudgels. And draw blood with the sword if that's ineffective. Damn." Ganto walked along the edge of the platform. "That detachment is sure taking its sweet time with whatever they're doing out there."

"Then we'll take up whatever arms we have," one of the nameless ones said, ignoring Ganto's present concern.

"And that leaves us right back where we started," Ageal interjected in Ganto's defense. "Facing a cruel and powerful military force while we remain inadequately armed and trained. There's no hope."

Ganto sighed. "Then that really does bring us full circle!"

"You mean with Joses?" another man among them clarified.

"That's right. And with his talk about nonviolent demonstrations that don't work. It's like protesting into the wind," Ganto said offhandedly.

"Which usually turns into a storm of violence against us that we cannot fight," Ageal said in support of Ganto.

"True. True," Joses conceded, his words drowning in a hail of verbal assaults. "Then call me crazy! But I'll not flee, either." There were some among the many that turned in Joses' favor. "I love my land. I love Israel. I love my God." The continued mix of changing allegiances and shifting disagreements turned the grumbling crowd into a caldron of voices. Joses was encouraged by all this uncertainty. "And judging by what I see here tonight, there's not a spy among us."

"Don't be so sure about that." Ganto glowered down at Joses, who stood near the edge of the platform near Ganto's feet. "Herod is very clever. His security system has managed to keep a tight control over us."

"Yeah, I'm always looking over my shoulder," one of the nameless ones added. His fervor infected several others into another vehement cascade of tense whispers:

"Son of a bitch! We've no say so in our lives!"

"Not without our farm lands!"

"That's right! Who can live on day laborer's wages or on share cropper's parcels!"

"Shit! I've been reduced to a vagabond. Never mind getting any work! Never mind—"

"Easy, men," Ganto cautioned. "Settle down. We're not fully out of danger, yet."

The men suddenly dropped to full silence again when the stable door was opened to allow Aher to enter. He quickly wound his way through the men to reach the foot of the platform near Ganto. "The detachment is gone."

In response to their general relief, the balance of the oil lamps and lanterns were uncovered. Then Judas was released from his pinned position and his gag was removed.

"Damn you!" Judas cursed. "All of you!"

Several men lifted him upward and set him upright onto the platform again with his legs and arms still bound. Judas was physically unable to do anything but maintain his uncertain balance. "I hate Rome as much as any man here. I wouldn't have alarmed them no matter what."

"You can't be trusted," Huri declared. "Not on any level. You're too inconsistent."

"Ganto and everybody knows that," Dathan added. "We don't know what you're going to be from one moment to the next."

"That's why we have to be rid of you," Ganto said. "Like a sickness."

"Like leprosy," said Balak.

Ganto looked in the direction where the court of seventeen roughly stood. "You've heard all the words. With a show of hands, how many of you think this gentile convert needs to be cleansed from us." All seventeen men raised their hands. "Hang him."

"Ganto, please!" the Pharisee finally shouted from within the swarming throng of men. "You can't!"

"Don't interfere, Rabbi." Ganto jumped off the platform to watch the execution.

Judas attempted to jump off the platform as well, but several men held him in check. Then Judas began to whine like an injured dog.

"Gag him!" Ganto ordered.

As soon as Judas was muzzled, Huri looped the noose around Judas's neck and cinched it tightly. He waited for Ageal to take the slack off the standing part of the rope by pulling it taut and tying it off to one of the stable's support posts, then he ushered everybody off the platform before he jumped off.

Judas was not a dignified sight. He writhed like a severed snake, shrieked through a mouthful of linen, and rolled his wide eyes like a mad man.

"Disgusting," said Ganto. Then he nodded at Huri, who tilted the platform out from under Judas's feet with the aid of two other men and pulled it clear of him.

The result? Silent stationary bystanders and silent squirming death at the running end of a rope. There did not seem to be a sense of satisfaction emanating from any of the spectators, including Ganto. No justice. No sense of revenge. Nothing. Just the approach of death—and the silence of its spectators, who still managed to enjoy the horror of this moment.

CHAPTER 6

Random Time, Random Place: Homeless Men

They lounged underneath the midmorning shade of a tree and tried to enjoy the best part of their day—a time when they were least harassed by hunger and thirst and discomfort. From this location, they'd watched three men crucified on Golgotha. The event was nothing spectacular. And since they themselves were nobodies, it was certainly not worth the danger of getting a closer look; to be a nobody was to be vulnerable to almost any class of men. Already damaged beyond repair, all either of these men had left to relinquish were their lives. And yet, because they were still blessed with some measure of hope, they chose to stay a few feet away from the ashes of last night's fire and, therefore, to remain within the relative safety of their cold camp.

They were a ragged pair of homeless day laborers—when they could get work, which wasn't often. But they tried—with dignity—they tried to maintain their self-respect. Both had once been reputable members of their villages. But taxes and debt, bad weather and bad luck, had destroyed their homes and their intelligent prosperous lives.

Their spirits sank to the bottom, however, when they were forced to beg for food or money. Although, to beg for work wasn't good for their morale either. They had managed to survive in the countryside for several seasons, then had migrated to Jerusalem to see if they could secure permanent work. But by that time, their wretched circumstances were reflected in their ragged tunics, their emaciated bodies, their bitter dispositions, and their desperate eyes. Elpaal, in particular, was unable to present himself well since he was coughing up blood on a regular basis and becoming more dependent on Pelet, who, although stronger, appeared to be on the edge of leprosy.

They were sitting on their threadbare mantles that were spread out like blankets on the ground; they had managed not to sell or trade their outer garments for food. Both men needed haircuts and baths, footwear and head cover, decent meals and medical attention—none of which they were ever going to get.

Elpaal coughed and rasped deeply, then spat a huge clot of blood on the ground.

"You need some medicine, my friend."

"I'm alright. Besides, how are we going to get medicine when we can't even feed ourselves." Elpaal was seized by another coughing jag. "I'd prefer a nice round loaf of bread."

"Yeah." Pelet began scratching the sores on the back of his left forearm. "Damn this itch."

Elpaal stood up, stretched, and studied the landscape of three crosses on the distant hill. "The poor bastards—especially Jesus."

"Especially nothing. They're all suffering equally." Pelet rose and joined Elpaal in studying the scene more carefully. "The branch of David will rule. What a joke." He spat on the ground to emphasize his distaste.

"He spoke of his lineage often, I grant you that."

"Then he must have been selling something."

"There are those who say he'll end the reign of Herod's unrighteous rule among us."

"With what? A kiss? Ha! How? By hanging on the wood? Ha!"

Elpaal began to wheeze with embarrassment, which forced him to reach for his breath as he spoke. "I've heard some people say he'll still liberate us from Rome's domination."

"You're not only sick, you're an imbecile. That's women's talk. Why don't you go join him at the foot of his cross." Pelet shook his head in dismay. "Elpaal, Elpaal, Elpaal. How can you destroy a foreign enemy with love?"

"I admit it doesn't make any sense to me but … but—"

"What. What!"

"When I was in his presence, somehow, somehow his words seemed clear and reasonable to me." Elpaal pursed his lips thoughtfully. "In weakness, power reaches perfection."

"Good Lord, now I've heard it all."

"I'm sorry, Pelet, I know it doesn't make any sense."

"It doesn't! I was there with you, remember? I heard the words, I . . . ahhh, I'm not worried." Pelet smiled. "Today's empty belly will remind you of your senses."

"Don't mock me, Pelet."

"And don't insult my intelligence. Ahhh, go on, get out of my sight, then. Go to the feet of your dying future king. But when your hunger pangs begin to gnaw at you tonight, see who's your brother then."

"Come on, Pelet, I don't mean to defect."

"Ahh. Hungry already?"

"You're making me angry."

"But I'm your brother," Pelet said mockingly. "And we have the one anointed by the Lord among us." He looked toward Golgotha. "Barely. Heaven—and the end of oppression and injustice and heathen rule is fast approaching us."

"God, you're impossible!" Elpaal was seized by a painful fit of jagged coughing, punctuated by the spitting of blood.

Pelet assisted his friend back to where their mantles were spread and helped him lie down. Then he sat beside Elpaal and waited for him to recover before continuing their conversation. Pelet tried to speak calmly and cautiously to keep from further aggravating Elpaal's condition. "It's God who's impossible if He expects us to destroy our rulers by the words out of His mouth. It's this kind of idiocy preached by those desert rats at Qumran that makes the reality of revolution impossible." A bit of ridicule slipped into the tone in his voice. "A ritual war against the Romans. Bah." Pelet pointed in the direction of Golgotha. "That lunatic has to be one of them." He tried to suppress the scorn in his voice. "If those Essene mystics expect God to defeat Herod's domination and Rome's tyranny or even eliminate whatever's left of Hasmonean influence by simply reading their war scrolls and avoiding any real military action, then those mystics are in for a long wait." He chuckled. "All but one of them, that is."

"That's not funny."

"Wasn't meant to be."

Elpaal rolled onto his side toward Pelet. "Besides, nobody's waiting for them to—"

"Then who? Another maverick sage? A Pharisee? Fat chance. They're no longer within any circle of political influence. All they have left is their piety and their Torah. They've no political voice. None! They're useless to the common man." Pelet pounded his chest with his fist for emphasis. "We're the ones who bear the direct burden of taxes and injustice and poverty. Both of our rulers have made criminals of us all. And as we stand before them as slave labor, their wealth grows before our eyes." Pelet remained quiet for a few moments, then he spoke slowly and deliberately. "As I've said before, it's God who's impossible if he expects us to destroy our rulers by the words out of his mouth."

Elpaal sat up. "He didn't expect us to destroy them at all."

"He? Who?"

"You know. Him."

"Aghh! So we're back to this damn Jesus again. And back to this sudden distrust of military force."

"I didn't say that," Elpaal wheezed. "I'm speaking of spiritual forces."

"Haven't you been listening to me? Haven't I been denouncing our present-day mystics?" Pelet redirected some of his exasperation by vigorously scratching the open sores on his legs. "Am I not also a child of Israel? Have I not heard the Psalms of Solomon? Damn this itching and burning. Have I not also waited for this . . . this teacher-king, this messiah who would succeed in establishing the true Kingdom of God?" He indicated Golgotha with his chin. "That man they've crucified is not the man. I'm telling you we must fight first before we can praise God later."

"He spoke of another kind of fight," Elpaal said, as if he hadn't really been listening to Pelet.

"Yeah, yeah, and he also spoke in parables," Pelet gibed. "I've heard even his close band of followers didn't understand him. Some leader he was if his own followers didn't know where he was taking them or why."

"Literal. You're too literal, my friend."

"Is it so literal that our own people oppress us?"

"Within your own question lies your answer."

"Which is?"

"To fight would simply replace one ruler for another."

"By God, that's the point," Pelet said excitedly. "To be rid of this line of Herods!"

"Our rulers before them were considered illegitimate by many."

"Who? By those crazy monk Qumranites?"

"And our Pharisees," Elpaal countered on the edge of another coughing bout.

"Priests. Priests. Our land is suffocating with priests! We are being strangled by this royalty. What we need is leadership—effective and real leadership."

"A new David, anointed by God," offered Elpaal.

"By God. By God?" Pelet stood up and strode a few paces toward Golgotha. "You really have been taken with that man."

"He could have been the one—"

"What? To lead?"

"No." Elpaal cleared his throat and spat out the blood that came up. "To rule an Israel empowered by God."

Pelet approached Elpaal and stood over him. "You're really not well, my friend."

"Now that's something we can agree on."

Pelet sighed. "I suppose they'll be calling your prophet a god next."

Elpaal shrank from him. "Be careful what you say, Pelet. Such blasphemy is dangerous even among ourselves."

"I'd like to see one of us enforce it."

Elpaal stood up to his threat. "Not me, Pelet. You know me." The fear of Pelet's size and matching brute strength forced Elpaal to regret his words. "Besides, if he were to proclaim himself a god, he'd be considered a mere lunatic among many."

Pelet backed away from Elpaal to reduce the tension between them. "Those are the first sensible words I've heard you say today. At best, he's a harmless lunatic." He laughed. "I like that. Rome shall be toppled and Israel shall be liberated by a dying lunatic. Oh brother. I really, really like that." Once again, Pelet directed his words toward Golgotha. "You better hurry up there, Jesus! You haven't much time to overthrow Rome!"

Elpaal inhaled deeply for the first time that morning. "Well, I can see there's no use talking to you."

Pelet waved his arms wildly about. "Talk. Talk all you want. Just don't expect to convince me that that lunatic is our royal Messiah who will unleash us from Caesar's rule or Herod's tyranny and prevent our next famine within the next few hours. That man is no key to our independence!"

"Politically? Perhaps not. Spiritually? Perhaps the key to . . . to the Kingdom of God."

"Bah! You're beginning to speak like one of those grateful slaves. Get out of my sight."

"I know what I'm talking about," Elpaal said defiantly.

"You're blind. You speak like a broken man. You speak without earthly hope. Go on, I say, get away from me. The afterlife is not for me."

"As you wish. I'll not take your verbal abuse any longer." Elpaal went over and picked up his mantle, shook it out, and threw it over his left shoulder. "But if you should change your mind later—"

"I'll not! Get away. Go to what's left of your Jesus. Go to your death you . . . you sick lamb."

Elpaal coughed spasmodically, regained respiratory control as he swallowed his own blood, and managed to address Pelet steadily. "I'll not be spoken to like that by you or by anybody else for that matter."

"Your increase in contradictions makes you more stupid than I had you figured. In fact, it makes me nervous to think back on our exploits together. To think I've actually trusted you with my life."

"And I trusted you with mine."

"Then don't. Not anymore," said Pelet. And in an attempt to goad Elpaal into anger, "Go on and join your merry band of idiots and women. See how far they'll get you once Pilate's no longer amused by their persistence." Pelet rolled his eyes suddenly, then looked up into the sky. "Look at me. What am I saying? Without your leader, the bunch of you will be like freshly beheaded chickens. His prophecies won't help you then." As if noticing Elpaal's presence again. "Go on!"

Elpaal began to leave, stopped, then anxiously turned toward Pelet. "You're wrong. You know that, don't you?"

"Maybe. Maybe not. But look elsewhere among the people in Palestine such as in Galilee and Perea and Judea. Look in villages such as Sepphoris and Bethlehem and Emmaus. Everywhere there are farmers and fishermen and peasants rallying around supposed anointed kings or princes. Jews everywhere live with the fire of hope. And everyone crazy enough to risk their lives and proclaim themselves a messiah have a quick and easy following:

followed by a swift and bloody retaliation as soon as Caesar or Herod or both smell real insurrection."

"Jesus wasn't like that."

"Yeah, well, he's dying a miserable death over there anyway—like the rest of them have—and will. Don't you see? There's no mercy among our rulers. Violent death awaits us all. You'll see. That—or you'll be dead by your illness first."

"I'm not a child. And I'll not be crucified as a thief, I promise you that."

"What does it matter, the reason. It will be unjust, nevertheless."

"It matters to me. It matters to me!" Elpaal coughed and hacked and spat.

Pelet waited for his sick friend to recover. "Let's see how proud you are when you're agonized by thirst and flies, by the heat of the sun and by the labor of your breath, by pain and humiliation and the desire of your own death before the wild dogs reach your stake in the night."

Elpaal pressed his hands over his ears. "Shut up, shut up, shut up! I'll kill myself first!"

"My, my, my. What a brave one you are who can't even stand to listen to the truth. You really do fit in with that weak and cowardly bunch." Elpaal approached him. "No, no. Stay away from me. I don't want whatever this disease is that you've caught from them. But I can promise you it's fatal."

"I'll pray for you, Pelet, if your time comes first."

"Save your prayers. I'll outlive you. And I won't be executed. I'll die fighting before I'll allow myself to be taken prisoner. I'll die a warrior's death, not a dog's." Pelet picked up his own mantle and began to leave. But he stopped, turned, and looked hard at Elpaal instead. "You are trying to balance too many contradictions, my friend."

"I . . . I can't help myself."

Pelet shrugged his shoulders sadly. "No matter. I fear you are not long for this world anyway. I . . . I can't help you any longer."

"I know. But in weakness, power reaches perfection."

"If you say so, my friend. But those words have the rattle of death."

Elpaal shook his head. "I know. I know."

Pelet sighed. "If it's any comfort: it's a bad end for all of us anyway." He left Elpaal standing miserably alone, his mantle still draped over his left shoulder as if he were going somewhere.

Elpaal's condition did not allow him to dwell on Pelet's abandonment, however. The sudden burning in his upper chest and his constricted throat forced him to cough deeply and painfully. He spat out another clot of blood, then sat on the ground beneath him, far too weak to go anywhere.

CHAPTER 7

The Second Watch: Lost and Found Conviction

"Crap. Cut the fool down," Ganto ordered. "This is no good. Quick. Cut him down before it's too late."

With the slash of a single dagger, Judas fell to the ground straining and writhing against his bound limbs, gasping and wheezing into his gag.

The only Pharisee among them quickly maneuvered through the knot of men between him and Judas. When he reached the agonized man, he knelt beside him, untied his hands, and rolled him to his side. Then he looked up at the toothless old man who had cut Judas down while he listened to Judas catch his breath. But his attention was averted by the hovering threat of the nameless man's weapon.

The object was not really a dagger, but a crude knife with a lethal point; the flat of it was scored by the owner's attempt to sharpen it against one of many desert stones. Its handle was fashioned out of two rough strips of wood made from a dead branch of a dogwood; a handbreadth's length had been cut from the branch, split in two, whittled toward some refinement, then used to sandwich the metal's squared end. These two pieces of wood were then held in place by tightly whipping a long lace of leather around the pressed together objects and threading the bitter end through the last three leather loops to complete the handle. It was not a handsome weapon, but it was a frighteningly effective one.

"Put that knife away," the Pharisee finally said as he untied Judas's legs.

"My, my, my," Ganto said facetiously. He'd been studying the Pharisee with an open display of contempt. "We are so blessed to still have a holy man among us so early on a Sabbath day—and during the Passover Festival no less. Doesn't this . . . this ministering to the injured on such a day violate some part of the Law?" The Pharisee turned to him as if to speak. "No. No. Don't answer that, Rabbi. Though, I'm almost curious how you saw fit to bend the Law of rest."

"I value justice as much as I do worship."

"Whoa. This man of God is showing teeth." During the crowd's interrupting laughter, Ganto noted the rabbi's increased somberness. "But please, I don't wish to offend you, Rabbi . . . Rabbi—"

"Elhanan," the Pharisee said. "I believe it's permissible to fight back in self-defense."

"Whatever you say. You're the learned legalist."

"No. Not very learned. Or very holy." Rabbi Elhanan looked at Judas, who was curled into a protective ball and trembling like a paralyzed wounded animal.

"Believe me, Rabbi, you wouldn't be among us if I thought otherwise," Ganto said.

"Say, who allowed this rabbi among us?" one of the nameless members of the crowd hollered.

"I did!" Ganto bellowed. "Your brigand chief."

"But he's not really one of us, is he?" another man remarked hesitantly.

"His hands have as many calluses as any of us. He works to eat if he's lucky." Ganto carefully surveyed the stable full of men to gain maximum attention. "Shut up!"

The rabbi stood up. "Thank you, Ganto. It's true I don't like this kind of man any more than you do. But it would have been unjust to execute him simply because he's different and confused—"

"And disloyal." Ganto's general contempt for Pharisees unwillingly peeked out again. "You rabbis slay me with your moral teachings. Talk, talk, talk. That's all it is. Even temple priests don't want to listen to your talk." Ganto shook his head disapprovingly as he watched the Pharisee kneel beside Judas again to check his condition. As Ganto's animosity increased, the Pharisee grew more prostrate, then seemed to imitate Judas's paralysis. "You and your kind who speak at the synagogues are out of touch with the people. You and all the others related to your kind with their heads buried in the Torah and other related scrolls. The Sadducees are corrupt, bought off by Herod and Rome. The Essene pious ones are too good for us and are constantly in their own minds—war scrolls my ass; ridiculous! And among them all there are scholars and teachers and scribes and lawyers tripping all over each other as they split hairs over the Mosaic Laws—and for what? What! Most of the people are us—ordinary and homeless and starving." The men cheered Ganto on, feeding his increasing resentment with their dissonant enthusiasm. "We can't read. We can't speak of the Torah except to mimic the words spoken by men like you, Rabbi." The Pharisee raised his head and exposed his blank face to Ganto. "We know the stories, yes. We know our festivals of thanksgiving to God, yes. We know how to pray—at least, some of us." This remark caused raucous laughter among the men. "But really, what are we? Jews who want to be left in peace with our families and our fellow villagers so we can work our father's land and live a life with God. But every time we turn around we are told by one priest that we must do this and are reprimanded by a teacher for our ignorance or are faced with these Greek and Roman pagans who are constantly changing our traditional way of life. We, the poor and the struggling, have to fight them all while burdened by taxes and tithes, by admonishment and disgrace, by laws and tyranny, by suffering and death."

"But these Pharisees often stand up for us," said Ithai, the young herdsman. "And you said yourself, Ganto, many are as poor as these men among us. Look at Rabbi Elhanan's calluses."

"I know, I know," Ganto said. "But mostly they spit into the wind with words that have no influence against our oppressors."

Aher stepped alongside Ganto. "Just like the Essenes who lock themselves away in their Qumran Monastery. They're useless to the ordinary man."

"Thank you, Aher. Like I said, all of them are useless in the face of our illegitimate king; he's a client of Rome! And all his priests act as retainers of his Temple government. I'd rather die fighting all of them in the hope for something better in my resurrected life."

"He's right," said Ageal. "Our new life has got to be better than this one."

"You don't have to convince us of that," a man on the edge of leprosy cried from the side of the stable near the horses.

Another man picked up a club. "I say let's give the next detachment of guards we see tonight a bit of their own treatment!"

During the general commotion and cheers and the frantic activity of those looking to find something that could be used as a weapon, Ganto indicated to Huri his desire to have the platform set right again. He leaped onboard as soon as it was firmly in place on its foundation of sawhorses and looked out among his people with his arms outstretched. "Wait! Wait! Are many of you prepared to die tonight?"

"We're all going to die one way or another," the leper cried.

"But without a purposeful cause," Ganto reasoned, "your death has no meaning. Don't you want meaning?"

"I want a full belly for a change!" Balak yelled. "And a roof other than the sky. And I want my children back and ... and— " He was overcome by the emotions caused by the recollection of his losses.

"Easy Balak, easy." Ganto waited until a couple of men had come to Balak's aid. "We've all suffered here."

"Yeah? Tell that to our Roman governor," a scarecrow of a man said with venom. "He had my father executed for not paying his taxes on time! 'Uncooperative,' Pilate said. 'Let there be a lesson in this!' The bastard!"

Judas stunned everybody into silence by standing up and speaking out defiantly. "You animals!"

"Well, well, well, Judas is back among us." Ganto walked the complete perimeter of the platform to increase the strain between him and Judas. "We're all desperate men. Life means everything—and nothing to us." Ganto noted that Judas was still massaging his throat like a hurt child. He shook his head, indicating disapproval. "You're soft. There have been too many women influencing you."

Judas had to clear his throat. "It was my Master's preference."

"Master, is it?"

"A force of habit, Ganto. The women among us seemed to worship him."

"Why?"

"Perhaps ... perhaps it was because he treated them as his equals."

"Ha!" Ganto said. Then suddenly baffled, "But why? To what benefit was there to that?"

"None that I could see."

Ganto walked toward the other side of the platform to gain a different perspective on Judas. "You're not holding anything back from me, are you Judas?"

Judas peered unwaveringly at Ganto. "I can't imagine what that would be."

"Hit him, Ganto!" somebody shouted.

Ganto raised his right fist to convey his annoyance and his demand for silence from the men in the pit at his feet. "Humor me, Judas. Bring him up here." He motioned the men near Judas to raise him onto the platform.

Judas resented his treatment as baggage. And as soon as he caught his balance on the platform, he approached Ganto. "I'm no jester."

"And I'm no wide-eyed child at the circus, eating sweet cakes."

Judas cautiously backed away from Ganto. "All I can say about Jesus that was particularly odd—above and beyond his other oddities—might be, might be—"

"Go on."

"He seemed to prefer—no—he seemed to have a number of women as close associates."

"But there was definitely a tight cadre of a dozen or so men who accompanied him most of the time." The attentive crowd of men quietly pressed closer to the edge of the platform as Ganto continued to speak. "You were one of those among them. Correct me if I'm wrong: weren't they always the same men?"

"Usually."

"And the women?"

"There were a number of ardent disciples who followed him, yes."

"More? Or less?"

"More and less."

"Don't play with my patience, Judas, or I'll hang you for sure."

"I don't mean to, honestly."

"Then out with it."

Judas wiped the burning perspiration from his eyes with the sleeve of his filthy tunic. "Jesus privately consulted with several loyal women, yes. Sometimes more often than with his loyal men. In fact, at times it was difficult to know who he considered to be among his specially chosen. It sort of altered a bit from village to village, town to town—even among shepherds and cattlemen and nomads in the open countryside."

Ganto seemed mystified. "Are you telling me he preferred the advice and company of women over men?"

"Sometimes more. Sometimes less."

"I told you don't play with me, Judas."

"I'm not!"

Ganto swung at the air with his fist. "Damn that man! He was no good to us. He was too ... too erratic. Too ... too unconventional to be useful. He diluted our military cause."

"The poor among us seemed to love him," Judas said without conviction.

"Bah! Why not? What's there to lose by not? Besides, I heard he was entertaining. That's enough for most peasants—believe me, I know. Hell, just look all around you. At your feet is the soil of Israel. I come from that soil. And to work upon it is a dull, backbreaking, tedious life."

"Then Rome did you a favor," Judas scowled.

Ganto grabbed Judas by the throat and forced him to his knees. "Your dark humor is not appreciated, you . . . you dried up turd." He released Judas, who remained on his knees gasping for air. The crowd of men maintained their silence—some even held their breaths. "Rome." Ganto spat on the platform near Judas. "Its taxes have personally cost me my land, my beasts, my children, my wife. Gone. All gone: either taken or killed. I would've paid them somehow. But Rome's not smart enough to wait. Oh, no! Rome destroyed me at the source: took away the possibility of next year by taking everything. Now they have no tomorrow to get from me and, still, only got part of what they wanted from me yesterday. They would have gotten their taxes! Now all they get is hatred from me as well as the burden of another bandit to deal with until I'm finally caught and put to death."

"I meant nothing by what I said," Judas rasped. "And I've tried to be loyal to you. I don't deserve this kind of treatment. Why didn't you approach Jesus yourself if you thought you could have done better? I'd have liked to have seen the result of your effort."

Ganto helped Judas to his feet and brushed a bit of the caked sand off of Judas's tunic. "My anger gets the better of me, sometimes."

Judas pushed Ganto's hand away. "And I'm sick of it. From everybody!"

"We needed you, Judas."

"For what? You should've seen for yourself that it was hopeless trying to recruit Jesus and his men—and his women. He was not a bad fellow," Judas said with a vague intensity.

"I wanted you to kill him when it became necessary."

"Why?"

"Because dying at the hands of Rome will make him a martyr. And that gives the people false hope."

"So?"

"Any hope is useless against—" Ganto bowed his head feeling the weight of his realization " . . . useless when fighting Rome."

"Then . . . then what are we doing?"

A nonplused expression spread across Ganto's face. "You can't be that blind. It's to the death, Judas—our death. Rage and anger is all there is because there's no real hope of winning. It's a bad end for all of us. It's only a matter of time." Somberly. "We are all slightly ridiculous."

"I'll not accept that."

"Then you're mostly talk, Judas. And you're a fool who doesn't belong here or anywhere else."

"Ganto's right!" one of the nameless ones finally hollered.

Ganto allowed the packed men in the stable to continue venting what they had to say:

"Even our own sympathetic scribes and Pharisees can do nothing but *mostly talk—and* interpret words and laws to a standstill—"

"Like Ganto said!" a beggar added, then peered at Rabbi Elhanan. "Sorry, Rabbi."

"*—and* are simply ignored by our party of Sadducees as well as our so-called King."

"We'll never get out from under all this oppression!"

"You mean, we'll never get away from this whirlpool of indebtedness!"

"There are even loopholes against the Torah's sabbatical protection!"

Dathan grabbed the edge of the platform and raised himself over its edge where he sat in order to gain more attention. He waited for the crowd to quiet down. "I remember there was a village with almost all its people reduced to tenants on their own lands; they fought back against our own aristocracy—even fought among themselves over petty debts. It got so bad that Rome stepped in, plundered the village, and crucified everybody."

Joses nudged his way through the crowd toward Dathan. "See? That's why Jesus said we needed to be kind to each other concerning the repayment of our debts to one another. We know Rome will never wait. And if we don't wait, we'll simply finish off those of us who are on the very edge of starvation—we'll destroy each other!"

"I've seen those kind of losses leave many, especially women, demonically possessed," said Balak, who was standing nearby Joses.

"It wasn't their fault," Joses said.

"Yes, well—say, who are you? Are you standing up for this Jesus?" Then Balak glared at Judas. "And this gentile?"

"Well, yes," said Joses nervously. "And I said it wasn't their fault."

"Tell that to one of our priests," Balak refuted. "To them these possessed of demons suffer because they've sinned—simple as that. Never mind the injustice and losses they've suffered at the hands of our oppressors."

"By our priests, yes," Joses said. "But not by our rabbis who live among us."

"The poor haunted bastards," Dathan said, ignoring Joses. "Can you blame them for their distress? Or their weakness and inability to fight demons? Other than death, what's left to them but this living hell? It's like a leprosy upon the land."

"Like you, Dathan!" one of the men in the crowd croaked, causing widespread laughter.

"But Dathan's right," Balak said in his defense. "They're not to blame. There are evil forces at work. Demons are as much to blame as our sins."

A general uproar of agreement erupted among the men.

Rabbi Elhanan broke through the crowd again, interested in Joses' defense of Judas. "I understand Jesus healed the sick. Did that mean he walked the countryside, forgiving people's sins?"

The men standing in the way of Joses and the Pharisee pushed and shoved each other until there was a clear path open between the two men.

"No, no," said Joses. "He was assisted by God in casting out demons."

"God? Are you sure?"

"It was God, Rabbi. Because it's God who forgives sins. Any man in his right mind knows that."

"Ahh, my point exactly. Was this man, Jesus, in his right mind?"

"Yes, damn it. Yes!"

The Pharisee approached Joses in an effort to reduce the tension between them. "It still seems like he could have been working for . . . for dark spirits himself."

Joses sulked momentarily before rebutting the Pharisee's statement. "I believe he worked for God the Father—he worked through His will."

"So you say, my son."

"So he said, Rabbi. My words are not hearsay. Where do your words come from since you've probably never been in his presence?" Joses didn't wait for the rabbi to respond—he turned to the crowd. "I say if this man Jesus can defeat Satan, the days are numbered for Rome. Israel will be restored!"

Some of the surrounding men jostled each other to maintain an open area for Joses and the rabbi—as well as a clear view—while most of the other men were simply satisfied to be able to hear the debate. To those who could see, the Pharisee seemed unconvinced. But for those who could hear, he seemed concerned.

"Okay," said the Pharisee, "if this rabbi . . . or prophet . . . or revolutionary, or whatever he's supposed to be was so eager to liberate Israel, what took him so long to get to Jerusalem? — the heart of Israel."

Joses ran his fingers through his hair in an attempt to control his frustration. "You know very well that eager is not the right word. And of what importance is the heart of the city when compared to the soul of the village?"

"Israel can't survive without both."

"You tell him, Rabbi," one of the nearby men said.

"Shut up and let them talk," said another.

Joses waited until he was sure he wasn't going to be interrupted by one of the spectators. "That might be true, Rabbi, but it's out among the people—those in the countryside, who are not twisted by the daily shadow of our Temple—where revolution really begins—"

"And probably ends among those lost sheep."

"Maybe," said Joses defiantly. "And maybe not." Joses was on the edge of anger. With a sweeping arm gesture, he presented the surrounding men to the Pharisee. "It's these lost sheep who pay for everything by the sweat of their brow. Few among them are wicked. And the simple fact is, there were fewer thieves and evildoers and adulterers than were said to have followed Jesus."

"I've heard the contrary."

"Then you've heard lies, Rabbi."

"Beggars and prostitutes—"

"Are not lost sheep—even though they're considered scum." Joses' statement caused a stir among the onlookers.

"You're not making many points among us, Joses," said Balak.

"Yeah, look around you," said another spokesman. "The homeless and the crippled, thieves and bandits—"

"Wait! I—you don't understand!" Joses said in a panic. "I . . . I was simply trying to make a point."

"Well, your argument has no flavor," Dathan joked. Uneasy laughter followed.

"And your point is pricking the wrong skin," Balak said. This time there were more serious murmurs of agreement concerning Balak's last remark amid the clamor and laughter.

"Alright, everybody, please settle down," the rabbi finally implored. "Please." The rabbi stroked his beard as he waited for the surrounding men to quiet down. "Very well, Joses," he conceded. "So Jesus was shocked by the hypocrisy found among our priests and scribes and scholars. Shocked by the lack of brotherhood among the people. Appalled by the declining morality of our age. But so am I! *So am I.* When has there ever been an overabundance of love among human beings?"

"You see?" Joses replied. "His point exactly."

"*His* point. His point? His point, it seems to me, is to discard everything for a love that cannot be counted on. An unconditional love that does not exist." The rabbi inhaled deeply before he released the full authority of his voice.

"That's why we have His Law. And God is a righteous judge who will reward the good and punish the wicked."

"Oh, really," Joses sneered. "And where's God's reward? Look—look around you. Do you mean to say that all of these men here lack the necessary virtue to avoid the punishment of poverty and homelessness, to avoid the pain of starvation and sickness?"

"I admit it's hard to fully comprehend the meaning of His Divine judgment," the rabbi quickly retaliated. "It's true: God reveals His will, but not Himself. It's you and I and everybody in here who must try to reveal ourselves— not God. True, this requires great sacrifice and faith. But sooner or later, the righteous will reap their rewards."

The following murmur by the stable full of peasants swallowed the ring that was left by the rabbi's last resounding statement.

Joses refused to be intimidated. "Then how does this conditional love differ from taking God's commandments with unconditional seriousness?"

The rabbi broke into a kindly smile. "This kind of seriousness is as close as we can get to God because man's love *is* conditional. That's what makes us human. Only God can be unconditional in His love. Only God. But you—you'll go mad if you try to express your love in this manner."

"But Jesus—he wasn't mad."

"Jesus, Jesus, Jesus," the rabbi reflected with some frustration, "he was one of us. A Jew. And his general message was in keeping with our teachings. He said so himself, right?"

"I . . . I suppose so."

"Look, I'll even concede that he was a learned Pharisee who lived and worked among the people, who read and taught in our synagogues, who even battled with himself over his contradictions—we all have them, you know." The rabbi noted Joses' confusion. "I've told you, I've heard about the things he's said. But I've heard nothing new. I've also been told about the rapture in his eyes. And all I can say is—" The Pharisee became concerned over Joses' growing distress. "Alright. Alright. I'll also admit that this man was an extraordinary healer among us. But . . . but what was the general meaning of his wanderings? What kind of example was this to our children? If what you say is true, he didn't seem to have respect for *any* authority—not just Roman or Herodian authority. How can the head of any household deal with such defiance to all authority?"

Joses seemed to be mystified by these facts as well. "It's true. He challenged all traditional authority."

"And the very fabric of the world—the family."

"Maybe."

"I'll allow no backtracking now," the Pharisee pressed.

Joses seemed stumped for an answer. And although he hesitated for quite a while, the spectators did not harass him. "Maybe he felt it was time to throw away all levels of authority."

"What?" The Pharisee looked at the surrounding men with amazement in order to maintain their support.

"Discard the levels," Joses continued. "Make authority—and God—available to all."

"But I'm the head of my household," said a one-armed man with a dark tumor on the side of his neck. "That is, when I had one."

"Then maybe it's time we change," Joses said amid the general clamor and commotion. "Authority makes masters and slaves of us all; it makes us no better than Romans!"

"You go too far," the Pharisee proclaimed.

Some of the men whooped to what Joses had said while others pushed past some of the weaker men to catch a glimpse of Joses and the rabbi. And while these spectators shoved and cursed each other for either a better position to witness this scene or out of plain disagreement, Joses peered up at Ganto, who was standing on the platform with one arm resting on Judas's shoulder. Judas appeared stoic and withdrawn, while Ganto was very much present and in control of this mock situation. The resentment Joses conveyed to Ganto with his disgusted expression made no impact on Ganto's cruel and aloof gaze.

Joses continued to speak as soon as the men settled down again. "This, I think, was the core of his revolution. Not just the release of the burden of our debts from our debtors, but the release of all masters—even the release ... the liberation from ourselves!"

"Try to sell that to the rich," one of the nameless ones grumbled. "They're without debt and, therefore, without sin. They are clean enough to rule. And that means God will support them."

"Not according to Jesus," said Joses. "Like I said, we are breaking under the demands of the rich—no—the master. So, in the spirit of what I heard Jesus say, let's discard the master."

The Pharisee was truly nonplused. "For God's sake, haven't you heard anything I've said to you—or Judas? Who are you?"

"I've already told you, Rabbi. I'm nobody. *And* I'm a brethren of Rabbi Jesus."

"You mean disciple."

"No, I mean, follower."

"Judas, it seems as if you've earned a temporary ally," Ganto finally announced.

The rabbi ignored Ganto and pointed an accusing finger at Joses. "Wide eyes. You have wide eyes. And you confuse slavery with the guidance of authority and practical Law. That's not revolution, that's anarchy. It's easy to discard, but what takes its place? If that's the so-called core of his revolutionary news then . . . then give me the words he uses from our very own scrolls instead: 'Love your neighbor as yourself,' and 'Love the Lord your God with all your heart, and with all your soul, and with all your might.' These are words that reflect the spirit of Israel. These are old teachings. Our teachings." The rabbi noted Joses' increased anxiety, then shook his head. "I'm sorry: he spoke as a Jew against his oppressor. He acted as a Jew toward his people. Jesus was a Jew who has said nothing new except . . . except for one verbal transgression I've heard about."

"And that was?" Joses interjected.

" 'To believe him.' No. 'To believe *in* him.' That's a very dangerous statement. And since I fear any serious conjecture on my part concerning this statement, I ask you: what does this mean 'to believe in him?' "

"That . . . that he's the Messiah?" Joses uttered cautiously.

"Are you asking me or telling me?" After a very long silence, the rabbi realized Joses was unable or unwilling to answer him.

"You've heard his words," Joses finally said. "You've heard his words. I . . . I don't understand. Why . . . why you're . . . *you're* so unaffected by them?"

"Would you have me respond like you? Or act like Judas?" The Rabbi grimaced. "I don't think so. But Jesus, well—we are of the same blood, nevertheless. He and I and you are of the same spirit; are of the same God."

"He has discarded the Law!" Joses blindly declared.

"No! No he hasn't."

Joses rapidly blinked his eyes in response to his growing agitation. "He said: believe in me! Because . . . because—"

"As I ask you to believe me," the rabbi calmly said. "As a teacher." He was becoming concerned by Joses' repetitiveness and increased irrationality.

"But . . . but you had to *be* there, I told you!"

"As you are here with me?"

Joses' eyes beaded wildly from side to side. "Jesus *had* an answer!"

"There is no single answer," the rabbi said with finality.

Impotence overcame Joses' ability to speak. He searched madly for a rebuttal, but it was beyond his reach.

The rabbi began to feel sorry for Joses. "My son, my son. I'll say it again and again and again and for all time if necessary: there's no dispute over the authority of Moses; or whether love of God and love of neighbor are firmly established in the Torah."

"You mean, no dispute . . . " Joses said tonelessly " . . . no dispute with Jesus."

"No!"

"Yes—no."

Joses' sullen response alarmed the rabbi. He suddenly grew concerned for Joses' overall darkening attitude. "I don't understand," he whispered gently. "What has Jesus said or done that seems so important to you?"

"Well he's . . . he's—*his* preaching gave those commandments greater status."

"You mean, he gave them another role in his preaching."

"Don't twist my words again, Rabbi."

"I'm sorry. I'm not trying to. Really," the rabbi said.

Joses' thoughts seemed to be unraveling. "You . . . you make what he did seem . . . seem so trivial."

"No, my son. Not at all."

"Rabbi Elhanan is a pious and honorable man," declared one of the ragged men. The overwhelming supportive response by the surrounding multitude embarrassed the rabbi.

By raising both hands, the rabbi made a humble gesture for silence. "Neither Joses' nor Jesus' moral conduct is in question."

"Then how else does that Galilean carpenter differ?" said one of the nameless ones.

The rabbi gazed at Joses with paternal eyes. "I cannot answer for you, my son."

Joses nervously licked his lips. "Well, his difference was not specific about everyday details, you see. His difference was something . . . something more general."

"Oh brother!" shouted a dwarf.

"No, listen," Joses demanded with the last of his strength. "Jesus did not exclude anybody—you included: *you*, who are generally ignorant of the Law. And in helping the likes of us—the common, the poor, the nobody—he refused any gain or pride of achievement. Don't you see? He was a righteous man."

"My son, my son," the rabbi said compassionately, "I never said he wasn't a righteous man."

"Thank you, Rabbi, for your wisdom," Ganto finally said as he jumped off the platform into the pit of men and approached Joses. "I guess I'm going to have to watch you more carefully." Then he circled Joses for dramatic effect. "You certainly waited long enough to explain yourself." He peered up at Judas, then back at Joses. "That makes both of you indecisive in character. Hmm." The men pressed closer together while managing to keep an open playing area for Ganto. He looked up at Judas again. "But as far as you're concerned, it's too late. You're doomed."

"But I didn't steal your silver," Judas whined.

"I know, you idiot. You misused it."

"That's not a crime worthy of much attention."

"It isn't one at all."

"Then . . . then what is my crime, Ganto?"

"What? What." Ganto chuckled. "You're damned, Judas. And you're a damn fool." Ganto looked into Judas's imploring eyes. "The answer . . . the answer is within the tone of your own question."

Ganto's cryptic statement, followed by his hard silence, paralyzed everybody in the stable into a breathless tableau. Only the horses could be heard shifting and snorting in their stalls.

CHAPTER 8
Random Time, Random Place: Men of God

They were old friends and ordinary potters by trade. But their pious demeanor and expertise concerning religious matters promptly revealed their highly regarded pharisaic status in Palestinian society.

Both men wore short-sleeved, knee-length tunics that were loose-fitting and stained with wet clay. Their heads were covered with full skull caps and their feet were protected by leather sandals; their beards were heavy and well trimmed and their fingernails were encrusted with the same brown material that was used to make the different types of jars, pots, and dishes as well as lamps, tiles, and storage bins.

Amos seemed worried. He visited Ben's shop to see if he had any overflow trade to pass on to him. Ordinarily, the steady flow of incoming pilgrims during the Passover week produced a great demand for oil lamps and, like his old friend, he had a special area set aside in his own workshop to produce mold-made clay lamps with his negative casts made of stone; it was the only easy money made through the course of the year, but, for whatever reasons, Amos had more lamps on hand than customers this festival period and no reason to make more until the thirty he had on hand were sold.

When Ben came to a good stopping point on the vessel he was forming on his potters wheel, he wiped off his hands on a rag and abandoned his work bench to give Amos his full attention. "I can sell your lamps on consignment, Amos. And, if necessary, send a percentage of my onetime walk-ins to you."

"Bless you, Ben. I wouldn't expect you to give up any of your regular customers."

"I know, I know. But if it came to that, I wouldn't hesitate to do it for a moment."

"Bless you again, my old friend. But I'm not asking you for that."

"Fine. Bring your lamps to me anytime."

"With the Sabbath at our heels, I'll bring some of them straight away."

"Fine." Ben noticed Amos hesitating at his shop's doorway and knew his friend well enough to ask, "Alright, what else is on your mind?"

Amos turned to Ben under the full weight of his thoughts. "Well it … shouldn't it be enough that we have to argue with our Sadducees concerning The Written Law of the Torah as well as argue for the validity of the spoken refinements surrounding the Law? Now it appears that this prophet, Jesus, actually wanted to disregard our whole body of wisdom and dismember our legal principles, one by one."

"I know, I know, we've been through this before." Ben's hands were still wet, so he wiped them against the sides of his tunic. "It's as if he supported ethical anarchy. Isn't that what we agreed?"

"Oh, but he didn't stop there, I hear. No. You know as well as I that the Sadducees might be against our system of teaching at the synagogues and are constantly posing questions against us. But what I've finally come to realize is that Jesus was prepared to tear down the entire fence around the Written Law, post by post and word for word."

"And judging by what you just said, you'd have almost thought he was in league with the Sadducees, but he wasn't."

"True. And you'd have thought he—well, who knows what he thought. He seemed to change his mind depending on who he spoke with. He certainly contradicted himself. And yet, he always seemed to be right. How did he manage that?"

Ben nodded his head and pressed his lips together to indicate his puzzlement. "I couldn't debate him. In fact, I confess: I wouldn't have dared."

"The Kingdom of God. Bah! Three years among the people and he almost . . . almost—"

"He lost his momentum, Amos. The people were turning away from him anyway. In fact, a favorable source informed me that that's why he brought his failing mission here to the heart of Israel. He had grown bitter and was throwing tantrums at his followers."

"He was mad. All he did was meet his end in Jerusalem. He must have known that would happen."

"Some say he believed himself to be the final prophet."

"Like I said, he must have been mad." Amos went to the shop's large water container for a drink. "First God's Kingdom was present among us, then it was almost at hand. It was sometimes here and sometimes there." He unhooked a cup from the side of the container, lifted the lid, and dipped out some water.

"According to him, God could be in both places."

Amos involuntarily sprayed some of the water he was drinking out of his nose and mouth. Then he coughed and cleared his throat. "Hmm. Clever." He coughed again. "Who could argue with him on that point? But . . . but is it possible? Can *we* be in *both* places?"

"According to him, yes—through God's forgiveness."

"That makes no sense." Amos reseated the lid and hung up the empty cup. "I swear, the man was possessed with the kingdom of madness."

"True. It does seem as if his before and after were no measure of His Kingdom's presence."

"His?"

"God's, of course."

Amos shook his head as he grimaced. "Too many contradictions for me. First, that Baptizer wanted repentance. Then, this prophet wanted . . . what? Change?"

"Conversion."

"To what?"

"To God's love."

"That must be earned!" Amos said angrily.

Ben raised both his palms at Amos in a display of innocence. "Hey, those weren't my words. According to him, it was free. It was already here. And it has always been here—available to all who'll listen."

"Preposterous, Ben. What about the Law?"

Ben went to the water container and drank a cup before he answered. "His primary Law was: love your neighbor. Therefore, to love your neighbor was to love God."

"But these are our teachings."

"Of course it is, Amos."

"Then ... then what kind of arrogance is this? Belief in God is it. That's all there is. That's all we can teach—right conduct is the path to Him."

"I know," said Ben. "Simply loving your neighbor is not enough. Good conduct must be taught and guided."

"That's right. Because the love of a madman is not necessarily good." Amos shuddered openly. "So ... so what did this man seek to accomplish?"

"To discard us, I think."

"But ... but why?"

"Well, according to him, the Kingdom of God—the Father—is already among us and available to everybody directly. To Jesus, we so-called go-betweens are not needed."

Amos shook his head with dismay. "But people need teachers and go-betweens to help them along. Besides, wasn't he a go-between himself? I mean—what manner of contradiction is this?"

"I don't know."

Amos firmly clasped his hands together. "Hmm. This man really was dangerous."

"Or really misunderstood."

"I swear, Ben, just when you think conditions in our land couldn't get worse—" He threw up his hands in a gesture of exasperation. "I think I prefer the woe that was typical of that beheaded Baptizer than to that crazy prophet's mad joyfulness and careless faith."

"Well, there's no joy in him now."

"Only the madness of his suffering on the wood," Amos said with genuine pity.

"The poor devil." Ben began to close up his shop. "Come on."

"What are you doing? Where are we going?"

"To the synagogue."

"At this hour of the day? And what about my lamps?"

"A prayer offering is the least we can do for a man of his religious attributes."

"But—"

"Your lamps can wait." Ben passed through the front entrance of his shop, unlashed his door, and held it open until Amos joined him. "He was a man." Ben shut and locked the door. "And therefore, one of God's creatures. Come on."

They headed down the narrow street and disappeared in the direction of their synagogue.

CHAPTER 9

The Second Watch: The Release

The men had taken a break from the formal setting of Judas's inquiry. Some of them had left the stable to find a place to relieve themselves, others were slaking their thirsts at the water jugs, while a few managed to get a second handful of parched corn. Small groups hovered near the light of their shared oil lamps in a haphazard pattern around the platform where Judas sat, dangling his feet over its edge, in the company of two guards. Within each group of men, a different debate raged concerning that evening's inquiry.

Independent spectators meandered from one group to another, listening and comparing the things that were being heatedly discussed. Among these mavericks orbiting the various groups were Rabbi Elhanan, Joses, and Ganto.

Each group approached a different aspect to the same subject—their miserable plight. And since most of them had nothing left to lose, this subject was endlessly fascinating and always worth repeating over and over and over, like a mantra of pain:

"Our sacred scriptures have no meaning to them."

"But it stands for our religion."

"Our government!"

"And our history."

"All three *are* inseparable."

"That's right. It's who we are—"

"*And* who we'll always be, by God—and to the death, so help me."

"Well, don't think Rome isn't aware of that. Why do you think they strengthen their garrison when we celebrate the festival of Passover? They know it's about liberation. They know we are fantasizing the idea of freedom. Why do you think these Romans are so nervous?"

"Because they fear us."

"That's right. They know, we know, what freedom means."

"Then why don't we fight!"

"Don't be stupid. Passover is an expression."

"Then what good is it?"

"It allows us to vent our distress."

"Big deal."

"And it liberates us in passing."

"You mean, it pacifies us like sheep."

"Maybe. But it also preserves our nation. Without it, we'd go mad. Without it, we'd fight Rome. Without it, Rome would crush us into oblivion, into nonexistence, into timeless history."

"Then what about this Nazarene who preached a new Kingdom?"

Joses had had enough of listening. He climbed onto the platform to draw their attention. "You idiots," he shouted unsteadily. "You idiots!" The multiple discussions among the small groups came to a halt as the men dissolved their cliques into a larger attentive mass directed toward the platform. "What do you think Jesus was saying when he declared the Kingdom of God was at hand? That's revolutionary talk. Haven't any of you been listening this night?" There were beads of sweat on his tense forehead. "It's plain and simple: God's presence among us now—here, in Israel—means the power of Herod and his high priestly clan, *and Rome*, are on their way out! That means revolution to the death."

"Unfortunately, at this moment, it's your rabbi's death," someone shouted.

"Yes." The remark hurt and disoriented Joses.

"Then what does that mean?" somebody else cried.

"I . . . I don't know," Joses muttered, no longer able to defend any position.

"But you do see where he's at," Ganto said, as he approached the edge of the platform. "Don't you?" Joses did not respond. "So, practically speaking, it leaves us with one man less to fight our enemy."

"That might not be true, Ganto," another man said. "Because did he really mean to fight Rome? I heard he never carried a weapon."

Ganto climbed onboard the platform. "Judas can verify that."

"He didn't," Judas said tensely. "But he was not without his anger or biting words."

Ganto was growing impatient again. "Only an organized armed rebellion will kill Romans."

Judas's voice developed a shrill tone during his response. "No, no, you still don't understand. Like Joses said, he was setting things up, you know, stirring the hearts of the people for a serious revolt—with God's help."

"We're all seeking his help," Balak shouted hatefully from within the crowd of men below. "But where is he, Judas? I want to be alive to see God liberate and renew Israel and bring salvation to the nations. Otherwise, what good is God?"

Judas was beyond exhaustion, beyond knowing what to expect. "My . . . my Master believed God had already started our political revolution."

"It's certainly not very far along."

"Ha! Good one, Jakim," said Balak.

Laughter spread raggedly toward the outer fringes of the crowd.

"But he was stirring the people's hearts," Judas continued, "open hearts made possible by our Lord's rule. This was supposed to lead to a real power change—a revolution."

"Listen to him," Joses cried, impotently.

"Shut up, you!"

"*Was*, Judas. *Was*." The men settled down with Ganto's somber interjection. "He's hanging on the wood now. You know, for one who didn't believe in his methods or ideas, you certainly defend him with great zeal." Ganto caught sight of Joses and glowered at him.

"That's right, Judas, you contradict yourself," Aher added in full support of Ganto. "Your actions say one thing and your words another."

"So? So, I contradict myself. Who in here doesn't?"

"Careful there," Ganto said. "You're getting too clever."

"Sorry. I was trying to mimic my Master's attitude."

"Your Master. That's not the first time you've said that."

Judas was startled by this observation. "Yes. Yes. I . . . I guess that's true."

From among the men surrounding the crude stage, a man quietly climbed onto the platform like a weather-beaten crab and stood beside Judas. Although the contrast between them was already startling, the man's coarse appearance became more pronounced by the involuntary tightening of his gnarled muscles.

Ganto sidestepped toward the farthest edge of the platform to give the man full command of the crowd, as well as to fully study him from a distance.

By the manner of his stance, he was a man used to girding the loins with his tunic in order to increase his physical strength as well as increase his freedom of movement while engaged in manual labor. The skin of his face, neck, and arms was as dry and cracked as sunbaked leather and his deep-set eyes noticeably lacked expression. There was little doubt that this man had fallen upon hard times; his grubby coarse tunic was in shreds and was gathered at the waist by a thin length of sash.

Although barefooted and bareheaded, except for a dirty wrap of a rag tied around his forehead, this man somehow managed to convey a quiet sense of plain dignity. "My name is Abiram. I'm just a simple man of the earth—once a farmer from the north." He slowly scanned the stable from right to left as if seeking a familiar face—even a friend. "I don't know a whole lot about a lot of things. But I do know Ganto. And I believe him when he says he doesn't care about what happened to the misused silver he gave Judas." Abiram paused to the general murmur caused by his statement. "And ... and, I also know Judas well enough to know that he probably didn't steal it." This time, he waited until the increased murmuring decreased on its own. "What I do know is this: Judas leads a careless life that keeps him in trouble."

"No more than the troubles you've suffered in your lifetime!" one of the men in the crowd hollered.

"True," Abiram humbly said. "I've lost everything I've labored for all my life. The grain from my fields, my olive oil from our presses, and the wine I managed to make wasn't enough to keep the tax collector from forcing me into debt. But that's not Judas's fault. He's one of us."

"No he's not!" shouted one of the nameless ones.

"I say he is—look at him." Abiram turned to Judas as if to encourage the others to see this man through his eyes. "Look. It doesn't take a genius to see that he's lost everything too. Look. Mud and dung have soiled his tunic. He's one of us: he carries the name and says he bears the scar of circumcision. More than that, he bears the weight of conviction—confused as it is. I ... well ... I feel sorry for him, that's all."

"You!"

"That's right, Dathan. And if *I* can, well ... well, that's all and ... and that's the truth." Abiram stepped off the table and dissolved among the many once again.

Ganto approached Judas from behind so he could push him aside. "Yes, that's all. But the truth is, Judas, you don't know what the hell you're talking about?"

"Maybe," Judas whispered.

"And the truth is," Ganto pointed to Abiram, "unlike that farmer who carries himself with great dignity, you keep going back and forth between truths—constantly keep changing your mind."

"Probably."

"In fact, you don't know what you are. And you can't be responsible for anything you say or do."

The flame of existence had gone out of Judas's eyes.

"The fact is," Ganto continued, "you can't be guilty of any crime since you're unsure of what your deeds are or should be. You're a pitiful mess! Not worth the trouble! Something that needs to be played with, tortured—then discarded."

The mob cheered at Ganto's last remark. "I've a better idea, Ganto! Let's cut his throat and feed him to the dogs!"

"He's not worth killing," Ganto bellowed. "No." He approached Judas and pushed him off the platform into the crowd's awaiting arms. "Throw him out into the darkness. He's guilty of nothing." He pointed down at Judas who was squirming along the top of a sea of outstretched arms and hands. "I sentence him to life—and death by his own hands. Throw him out of here."

"No, Ganto, wait!"

"We've heard enough of you, Judas. Throw the bastard out into the darkness, I say!" Ganto watched Judas float along the top of the crowd toward one of the stable doors. He squirmed hopelessly against his fate. "This might not have been the Court of Seventy, but I condemn you, Judas. I condemn you to live long enough to take your own life. You're a traitor to the Jewish cause because of your unaccountable thoughts and deeds, your inactions and shortcomings and stupidity. You're not one of us."

"I'm not a pagan!" Judas shrieked as he struggled against the arms and hands that brought him near the open door.

"No, you're nothing, you ridiculous bastard! And you're unwanted! Your continued existence among us can only cause us more pain and suffering. Hurry. Get him out of here before whatever sickness he has continues to spread." Ganto peered at Joses. "There's probably already one among us who's already caught this sickness." Then Ganto glanced back at the stable's open doorway just in time to see Judas being thrown out into the night.

CHAPTER 10

Random Time, Random Place: Among Disciples

They stood facing the open road on the outskirts of the village they had just left. They were tired from their day's journey, but relieved that the people in this locale had been generous to them—spring had provided an abundant harvest of flax and barley this year. Their sacks had been filled with leftover flat cakes and second-rate cheese, several garlands of dried figs and a generous helping of olives. And although wine was not offered, they'd been encouraged to borrow a couple of containers full of fresh water—to be returned the following morning.

Always three, only three were chosen to enter any nearby village for alms and return with what was offered. It was the hardest part of the day: the tail end, when hunger and thirst and the weariness of the road had its greatest detrimental effect upon those who followed Jesus throughout the countryside.

Two of the three men were strongly built; both had once been fishermen who still showed signs of their trade even after almost three years away from this occupation. True, their hands were no longer callused or cut and their muscles were no longer knotted or sore by the long laborious hours of pulling in dragnets or casting shallow water nets or simply pulling on boat oars, but their wide gait and their stooped shoulders clearly marked them as watermen. Both of them wore a lightweight upper mantle over a simple skull cap and a shapelessly styled coat over a thinner tunic, which covered their encroaching gauntness that was on the verge of ravaging their sturdy physiques. Both men were fully bearded and carefully groomed despite the hardships of constantly living on the road.

In direct contrast, Judas's slight figure was a bit dwarfed alongside these men. But the intensity in his eyes and the aggressiveness in his overall demeanor made him equally formidable in presence.

"There's been more talk about your conversion."

Judas turned squarely toward Thaddaeus. "And what of it?"

All three of them relieved themselves of their burdens by lowering the food sacks and water containers to the ground.

"Well, even these villagers can see it."

"So? Palestine is filled with Greeks and Syrians, Idumaeans and Galileans, Samaritans and Judeans, Egyptians and—"

"Yes, yes. But still—"

"What? It's true, I'm an Israelite by choice."

Thaddaeus peered at Philip. "See? He's not one of us."

"Not by blood, no," Philip said. "But by mind and spirit, yes. And these could be even greater bonds, perhaps."

"That's possible. I won't deny that." Thaddaeus licked his lower lip. "But I won't accept it, either!"

Philip placed his left hand on Judas's shoulder to keep him in check. "Control yourself, Thaddaeus. All this is old news. Why do you persist in this rivalry with Judas? Like us, he's trying to seek out the truth."

Thaddaeus scoffed at both of them by kicking up some dirt. "Whatever that is. I neither understand our Master nor trust this . . . this Corinthian gentile convert. I don't understand it. And I don't like it."

"Please, enough of this, Thaddaeus."

"You speak openly in his defense. Why doesn't Judas speak for himself?"

"I'll speak—I've nothing to hide," Judas said. "And I'll not speak—I'm prepared to fight. Choose either. I'm ready."

Both Judas and Thaddaeus squared off in a threatening manner.

"Stop this, both of you!" Philip demanded.

"Judas is the violent one."

"I won't deny that my sympathies and past alliances have been with the aggressive freedom fighters."

Thaddaeus glared at Judas. "Sympathies. Freedom fighters. More like hungry bandits and marauding thieves, if you ask me."

"I'm not asking you."

Thaddaeus remained unafraid of Judas's threatening tone. "Then, perhaps, I should—"

"I said stop this!" Philip maintained his stance between them, angered by their pettiness. "Thaddaeus, take up your sack of food and one of these containers and go see to our Master's needs. Go on."

Judas waited until Thaddaeus left before uttering his disparaging remark. "He speaks like a Roman sympathizer."

"You ought to know better than that."

"I wouldn't be surprised if he were carrying some of Herod's silver, as well."

"I said stop it, Judas! You're going too far."

"I can't help myself. He infuriates me. And I can fight my own battles, thank you."

"Precisely the wrong words, Judas. And what I was afraid of. You really need to change your views—your attitude."

"This is a revolution," Judas said intensely.

"No. This is a new spiritual movement and . . . and a political protest and—I'm not exactly sure what it all is really, except, these things are not separate from each other or the Kingdom of Heaven."

Judas assaulted Philip with a smug expression. "Then you don't understand our Master anymore than Thaddaeus does."

"And it's obvious you don't, either."

"I don't want to."

"How can you say that?"

"I have my own reasons."

"And it's dangerously violent. It's a sure method for losing one's life."

"At least something would be happening," Judas said snidely. "Turn one's cheek. Love your enemy."

"These are not abstract truths, Judas."

"Oh, no, not according to our Master," Judas added facetiously.

"But he's right. If we didn't turn our cheeks, the Romans would simply kill us."

"Then I'll take death—"

"By violence. Like, for example, with Simon."

Judas peered at Philip hardheartedly. "So?"

"Don't you see? If we didn't at least act as if we loved the enemy—"

"Damn Romans—"

"Alright. The Romans. They're one enemy. And without at least a pretense of love for them, we couldn't very well be sincere about loving our own enemies."

"Our own?"

"Yes. Within. Among us. Our fellow villagers who are in great debt and in great threat of starving and of becoming homeless—always homeless."

"I . . . I don't understand. What's your point, Philip?"

"If we vent our frustrations against each other by attacking one another, then . . . then the Romans win again."

"I'll not be slapped by Thaddaeus or anyone."

"Judas, Judas, all our Master is saying is if we continue to retaliate with violence against one another, all we can do is draw more attention to ourselves. Rome will not—does not—tolerate disorder, you know that. If we persist in violence even among ourselves, Rome will increase its repressive rule. And that means a swift sharp sword. They've no heart, Judas, you know that. We are hated. They would just as soon kill us as enslave us. Our suffering doesn't matter to them. In the end, they'll crush us."

Judas crouched down with frustration by the remaining jug, poured water into his cupped hand, then splashed it against his face. "But ... but something's got to happen, something!"

Philip knelt down beside him with pity. "And what do you suppose is happening when our Master heals the sick, fills the hungry, empties their torment by casting out demons?"

Judas stood straight up. "I haven't come this far to become an itinerant quack healer. And to make things worse, he gives away most of our money and food and then expects me to feed your hungry mouths when we've come to our place of rest for the night."

Philip drank some water before he stood up. "We do alright."

"I hear complaints all the time."

"Forgive them."

"Easy for you to say. You don't have those damn fishermen—no offense to you intended—breathing down your back every evening, anxious for something to eat and drink."

"They're only human."

"And I'm not? I've not had a decent meal in weeks. Months even. It wears a man down."

"It seems to strengthen our Master."

"Why shouldn't it? He seems to get the choicest portions."

"Perhaps—wait—no, that's not true."

"Sometimes I wonder which one of us is the lunatic."

"Judas! He's our Master."

"Yes, yes, and I'm his slave. Or so it seems."

"Look, Judas, my friend—I'm unsure about things myself, sometimes. Living in the streets, wandering in the countryside, withstanding cold and hunger and uncertainty."

"Why do you stay then?"

"Why?" Philip was at a loss for words momentarily. "When I look into his eyes, there is no why. When I feel his nearness, cold and hunger seem irrelevant—even welcomed."

"You can't always count on his presence. He will leave you someday. Or you, he. Then what will you do?"

"I ... I don't know. But ... but I do know he speaks a lot on the self-sufficiency of faith."

"Bah."

"Faith, Judas. Whatever that is, I know it's the key. It's the spiritual nourishment he speaks of, that I hunger for—that I lack. I know that: I cling to him far too closely not to know that."

"You big baby."

"I don't deny it. I don't deny anything. I don't know enough to even consider denial. But you. What do you deny? Most of all, why do you stay among us?"

Judas coughed uncomfortably. "You think I'm not split with doubt, either?"

"Of that, I'm sure of. But into what parts?"

Judas clenched his hands together to release some of his anxiety. "More than two, I can assure you that."

"That's for certain."

"Certain?" Judas almost laughed. "And what do you really know about me?"

"A man learns a lot about another man after sharing with him his daily measure of hardship and hope, after listening to his evening's snoring and scratching, but most of all, after watching him respond to our Master's affection: his words and deeds."

"But it never lasts," Judas said with fierce intensity.

"What?"

"His affection. The feeling of his affection. It dissipates with the day-to-day struggle, with the tug of so many sick and needy people, with . . . with the cold misery of life, damn it!"

Philip patted Judas on the back. "That's why you're one of us."

"Oh, Philip, don't give me any praise. It's undeserved. My motives . . . my motives are not of the spirit."

"You're too hard on yourself, Judas."

"I'm just a realist. I'm a revolutionary filled with hate for his enemy. Not love, Philip. Not love like our Master preaches."

"But as I pointed out to you earlier, Jesus is also a practical man. To turn your cheek and to love your enemy—remember? These are difficult, yet, practical advantages for survival. Not just spiritual talk."

"That's what you say."

"I know, I know. It seems hard to accept—even harder to understand. Believe me, I find myself hating, too. But when I listen to the revolution that he speaks of—its freshness, its impossibility, its radical difference to all the other revolutionary failures of man—I realize his love must be the answer. It must be, impossible as it seems."

"Bah!" Judas knelt on the ground, opened the supply bag that was his burden, and rummaged through its contents momentarily. He pulled out a stack of flat bread and sniffed them. "Stale. All of it. It makes me crazy, sometimes." He threw the stack of cakes back into the sack. "At least the sword gives some comfort to a man in his failure."

"But why always see it as failure?"

Judas slowly stood up. "Because life *is* failure. And it's just as well that we die like men. Maybe that's all we can expect."

"I hope not, Judas. For your sake. For my sake. For the sake of all living beings—we must follow his example."

"Like I said, I'll not end up a starving magician."

Philip was finally struck by Judas's persistence, startled by his denseness. "My God. You really don't understand what this . . . what he's about."

"I can point the same sincere finger at you."

"Maybe Thaddaeus has been right all along: you don't belong among us."

"It's our Galilean wonder worker who'll not be among us much longer if he keeps up with this unarmed resistance." Judas grimaced. "Love your enemies: it's women's work."

"I'll admit it's a strange sort of aggression to provide for each other in the face of Rome, especially if the fellow villager who needs assistance is someone you despise."

"Strange is an understatement."

"Alright, a difficult kind of unity against our enemy."

"Impossible, you mean."

"Judas, please, beware of what you seek to do among us."

"Don't worry about me. I know what must be done even if this ... this man doesn't."

"Judas! Please. You speak so ... so distantly of him."

"He's a man."

"Judas."

"A clever man."

"After all you've witnessed?"

"Alright, alright, a great man."

"And our Lord."

"Yes, yes, a king from the House of David. Fine. He made that abundantly clear. And you. That must make you a prince since you're his stepbrother."

"I wouldn't know about that," Philip said defensively.

"Don't insult me. You want your own royal throne. You want to be . . . to be sure you maintain your rightful place in line to claim your kingdom."

"But only God has the power to claim—"

"Yes, yes, please, I know the words. Feed them to the deaf and dumb. Brother—what a flock. Losers. All. I can't believe you've turned against me, Philip."

"No I haven't."

"But you're even defending Simon against me."

"For you, Judas. For you. I believe that's what our Master wants: for us not to act with self-destructive violence."

"Nonsense. Once blood is tasted, its lust will always return."

"Perhaps. Perhaps not—with his help."

Judas strode several steps away from Philip, filled with exasperation. "I can't believe you've fallen prey to all this simplicity."

"Our Master speaks from the heart. He speaks to mine."

Judas turned toward Philip and approached him as if it were an attack. He grabbed Philip's forearm. "You're my only ally. I need you."

Philip pulled his arm from Judas's hold. "I want nothing to do with simple banditry. It's a dead end. Rome will completely destroy us if we persist. Look, even Pilate has responded to our people's nonviolent protest."

"Sure. Occasionally. But look at what price!"

Philip's exasperation was getting the best of him. "I want no more of this."

"Listen to me—"

"No! Listen to him. Not yourself."

"You're a traitor, Philip."

"And you're a deceiver. You're no true follower. You're a mercenary, an opportunist."

"Then why haven't you made that known?"

"Because . . . because it's not our Lord's way."

"Crap. Words from the king again. Drool. Drivel," Judas said with increasing venom in the tone of his voice. "I don't care what anybody thinks, but slap *me* in the face and I'll . . . I'll kill you."

"Judas, listen to yourself! You're no longer in touch."

"Oh? And what does our Master touch with his words?"

Philip's voice cracked with hesitancy. "He touches what concerns daily existence."

"Of peasants."

"Of course. He speaks of hunger, poverty, and grief."

"Among our people."

"Of course. He speaks against hatred and ostracism—you know that."

"Brother. For a man without understanding, you certainly seem to have a lot of answers."

"Say what you will, Judas, I'll not try to support you further."

"Good! Then leave me be."

"Judas—"

"Go on! I don't want to hear you. I'm alone. Alone!"

Philip shook his head. "Alright. I'll not argue with you anymore today."

"Good. Don't. See if I care. Ask me, go on. Ask me if I care."

Philip picked up his sack of food and the remaining jug of water. "I'll ... " Judas turned away from him and openly ignored him. So, in an effort to control his anger, Philip stomped away from him. "I'll not keep the others from this food and water."

Judas waited for Philip to be well on his way before he turned back around. He wanted to call out to his only friend, but something prevented him. He saw a loose stone on the road, kicked it, and hurt one of his toes in the process.

CHAPTER 11

The Third Watch: Bearing the Cross on a Jerusalem Street

In the wake of all the physical and mental abuse he suffered at the hands of his so-called compatriots at the herdsman's cattlefold, Judas stumbled within Jerusalem's darkness without direction, yet, knowing deep within himself, to what end his life was taking him—he was afraid: Ganto's condemnation rang in his ears.

The stench of the empty streets was particularly distasteful this evening, particularly since the spatter of urine was soaked into the lower hem of his tunic and the buildup of animal feces was encrusted between his toes. He was a mess and he knew it. Even the gatekeeper had avoided any verbal contact with him in order to hasten his wild-eyed passing.

Judas had been found not guilty. But he was mad with guilt. Mad!

"Away, demon! Leave me be! Stop torturing me for the sins of others. I am free, free of any debts. Away, demon!"

Judas pawed at his breast as if he were trying to rip the evil force from his body. He would have torn himself to pieces if he could have in order to release himself from the bonds of his misery and torment and increasing disorientation.

He saw a pair of frightened eyes illuminated by a weak chink of light through the opened crack of a shutter.

"What are you looking at!"

The shutter snapped shut just as he attacked the window with his fists. He pounded on the rough wood until he drew blood. Then he stopped to look at his torn hands and began to laugh at the lack of sensation in them; he felt no physical pain.

He stumbled down a long narrow alleyway until it met a crossing street that he recognized. Judas became frightened by its familiarity and by where this recognition was going to lead his thoughts. He didn't want to remember. He didn't.

He began to run, but physical exhaustion prevented him from traveling very far. He collapsed at a place where three streets came together. It was where Jesus passed him on his way to the place of crucifixion. Judas pressed his face down into the dirty street and sobbed.

When the wells providing him with tears were finally depleted, his consciousness began to drift into and out of the present. He wanted sleep. Sleep! What he got, instead, was the passage of time and space into that condition often called a dream state. But Judas had actually been there, had seen his Master's suffering for himself. So, where did the reality of life end and the condition of dreaming begin? And where was this separation, this interruption between life and dreaming? Did dreams interrupt life or life interrupt dreams?

Again, his body fought desperately for sleep, but his mind forcefully thrust him into dreams:

Judas raised his head and squinted at the harsh glare of the hot sun. The jeers of a cruel mob assaulted his ears as he saw a pair of bloody uncertain feet stagger to a halt. He raised his head up higher and discovered that it was his Master. The sight of him cut his heart in two.

Both fresh and dried blood covered Jesus from head to toe. His skin glistened with it, his ragged tunic was stained with it, and his hair was matted with thick clots of it as well as freshly soaked by it because of a plait of thorned branches that had been brutally pressed onto his head.

Judas stood up to meet the misery in his Master's face. The horror in his uncomprehending eyes almost forced Judas to flee. His Master tottered sideways a couple of steps. Then he planted his feet squarely on the ground in an attempt to regain his balance, which brought the slow procession to a halt. But this effort for control failed and Jesus fell under the heavy weight of the stout cross beam he was dragging: first to his knees, then fully prone with his face pressed into the dusty street.

Judas could see the concern in the centurion's expression: this weak man threatened to perish before reaching his appointed destination. The centurion reigned his horse around in Judas's direction and commanded, "You. Come out here and help this man."

Judas quickly stepped forward, grateful for the opportunity to be close to his Master.

"No, not you," said the centurion. "Him—the big one."

"Me!" said the man.

Noting the anxiety in the man's voice, Judas turned and recognized that it was the man who'd been standing beside him. He was a broad shouldered peasant who looked to be a Cyrenian Jew by his dress.

"I can assist him," Judas nervously volunteered.

"Thank you, brother," the Cyrenian said.

"I said the big one," the centurion said. "You. What's your name?"

"Simon."

"Take up this man's cross beam before he dies under its weight."

Simon shot a furtive glance at Judas followed by an anxious whisper. "My God, I hope I'm not mistaken for one of his followers and crucified along with him."

"What was that?" the centurion demanded.

"He told me he's glad to be of any service to Rome," Judas said. "And so would I. So, please, please let me volunteer my services to this man."

"I said get away, you!" The centurion nodded to one of his legionnaires who wasted no time in implementing the silent order. The legionnaire attacked Judas with a bludgeon and struck him down with several blows to the head and shoulders and back. He left Judas sprawled face down in the street. Still conscious, Judas lifted his head and looked at Jesus who was lying at the same level only a few feet away, his head tilted up in order to face him.

"Was I chosen for this?" Judas asked.

Jesus looked at him with eyes that seemed to say, yes.

"I . . . I had mixed and confused intentions from the beginning."

Jesus raised the index and forefinger of his right hand in a gesture that seemed to convey forgiveness.

"But you said yourself: it would have been better if I'd never been born. You did say it, didn't you? Or did I think it aloud?"

The legionnaire assaulted Judas again for good measure. "Shut up!"

"Out of the way, the rest of you!" the centurion said to the mob while two other legionnaires helped Jesus onto his feet. Judas managed to crawl toward his Master, but when he reached out to touch him, the centurion started the procession moving again by leading the way.

The crowd enveloped Jesus and the Cyrene bystander, who had lifted the crossbeam off of Jesus and thrown it upon his own back, obliterating his Master's figure from Judas's eyes. He knew it was the last he would see of his Master, the last words they would share. The weight of his misery forced Judas to lower his head, where he discovered an image cradled in his arms before him; it was his Master's blood-stained face imprinted on the ground! He went mad with tears. Then Judas pounded his own lacerated face against his Master's image until there was nothing left but a muddy mixture of blood and dirt on the street and until he was unconscious—and unconsciously driven into another dream:

Judas crawled to the foot of the cross and touched the base of the wooden stake. "What's my guilt? Why do I still cry out in pain to you? I've been exonerated by your—our people. I've been taken among them, judged, and have been discarded back into the sea like an unwanted fish. Unwanted. I'm unwanted and hated! Please, please forgive me, Rabbi, I know not what I do. Forgive me." He was startled by the rough tongue calling down to him. It was a voice other than his Master's.

"Get this crazy idiot away from me!"

Judas lifted his head, focused his eyes, and saw an unfamiliar man: tortured, naked, and nailed to the wood.

"Azriel, who is that?" another voice cried from above and behind Judas. It must have been the other man who'd been condemned to die with his Master. "Azriel?"

"Forget it, Nikos! That piece of shit at my feet is not one of us!" Azriel looked down on Judas. "Get away, you! Damn your eyes for awakening us back into our torture!"

Judas felt a sudden excruciating pain in his side. He turned his head and discovered a Syrian guard standing nearby.

The guard kicked him in the ribs again. "Get off this hill or you'll join them in their suffering."

Judas began slithering away on his belly, unable to acknowledge the order, since the wind had been kicked out of him. However, his departure apparently wasn't quick enough. He received another kick from the guard, which forced him into a sideways roll down the modest hill of Golgotha. He flopped to a standstill, where he curled into a ball on his side, then drifted into another unconscious timelessness:

Like stone statues, two frightened figures stood pressed against the damp wall of a Jerusalem alleyway, almost afraid to breathe while facing the bizarre darkness of fear and trembling.

"Now you're no better than I," Judas whispered vehemently. "You deserted him."

"I was afraid," Philip said. "Where ... where are the others?"

"Scattered: arrested, running, in hiding. At least I stood between him and those legionnaires."

"Don't boast, Judas. You kissed him. I saw that."

"At least I stood my ground. What say you, hypocrite? Where's his Kingdom of God now?"

"You're too unkind, Judas. You've walked with us. You've heard his words with your own ears. You've dipped your bread in the same bowl. You know the mystery."

"And understand nothing. Nothing!"

"Shh, not so loud. I'm not speaking of understanding."

Judas exhaled as if for the first time after reaching that deserted alley. "He was a magician, I tell you. An enchanter."

"How can you still say that, my brother? You ... you drank from his own cup."

"Then why are you leaning against the same wall alongside me?"

Philip pressed the back of his head against the wall, feeling the full weight of his shame. "Being a coward has nothing to do with the legitimacy of our anointed Master."

"Legitimacy—"

"Shh."

Judas hissed through clenched teeth. "Where's his influence now?"

"A shepherd and his flock must—"

"Sheep. That's right. We're sheep. And now that the shepherd's gone, look at us and the rest."

"It is he who's the lamb of God."

"Then sacrifice yourself as well, if you've the stomach for it," Judas whined. "But I don't think so. Scatter. Go on. Continue to show your disloyalty like the sheep we are."

"Not fair, Judas."

"Fair! What's fair! Believe or disbelieve. What does it matter? Look at us: we're frightened losers seeking the shelter of reassurance. But you'll get none from me."

"Judas."

"Go on. Seek the others. I had reasons for what I tried to do. I had reasons! The rest of you deserted him at the hour of his greatest need like swine."

Philip verbally struck back with what he had perceived. "You betrayed him with a kiss."

"Ridiculous. I protected him from the daggers of my fellow countrymen. He was going to be arrested anyway.

Good thing, too. One of those daggers would have found his heart."

Philip was horrified. "You don't mean——"

"He would have been assassinated on the spot if it hadn't been for my kiss. What good would that have been politically? Tell me."

"He talked of heaven among us. He was a visionary—a true revolutionary."

"An arrest should have caused greater numbers to come to our allegiance. Greater numbers, Philip. Not the paltry hotheaded few we'd have gained by witnessing his assassination. Bah. You. All of you make me sick."

"So where are these greater numbers?" Philip demanded. He waited until he was certain Judas was unable to answer him. "Well, I'll tell you. They're against other walls like this, that's where."

"Alright, alright, so I've misjudged our people's potential."

"You're wrong, Judas. The truth is, you've been used. And your thoughts . . . your thoughts are always in a muddle. You don't know who you are, but . . . but I forgive you."

"I don't want your forgiveness."

Philip finally pushed himself away from the wall and started backing away from Judas. "It's done, whether you like it or not. It's done: you're forgiven." Philip disappeared into the darkness.

"Wait. Philip. Wait! What does that forgiveness mean? What does it mean?"

Silence was his answer.

Judas inhaled with a start as his eyes fluttered open: the street was barren. All that was left was the truth of darkness that bridged life with death, connected the flow of wakefulness with the dynamics of unconsciousness, and obscured the apparent separation of reality from the world of dreams. The darkness from one was no different from the darkness of the other: there was no difference—nothing. Judas closed his eyes and drifted toward another form of unconsciousness and, therefore, into another form of nothing.

CHAPTER 12

Random Time, Random Place: Two Scribes

They stood in the immense outer Court of the Gentiles amid the din of activity: moneychangers at work, merchants selling sacrificial animals, pilgrims meandering in and out of various porticoes listening to teachers preach and scribes argue over the fine points of the Law—everywhere one turned there was activity and sun and talk.

One of the two scribes standing together was ancient and the other was very young—in fact, by scribal standards, barely an adult.

Although the day was warm and bright, the old scribe wore a long outer robe, opened in the front, over his full-length tunic. His head was covered with a full turban and his face was adorned with a long beard. He stood with some difficulty and with a slight list to his right because he leaned on a cane for support.

The young scribe also wore a full-length tunic. But he wore a mantle, loosely draped across his left shoulder and wrapped around his right side, with four blue tassels sewn to the hem. His beard was sparse, his hair longish, and his head covered with a full skull cap.

It was a glorious day within the walls of the outer court, but both men were too mentally preoccupied to notice. In fact, their hesitancy about entering the inner courts while still engaged in the present subject of their private conversation was the only reason the sun was still shining on their backs.

The old scribe placed his free hand on the young man's shoulder. "I hear this Nazarene you've spoken about treats women as his equal."

"He respects their own brand of authority, allows them the role of partner, even treats them as disciples."

The old man was startled. "Who in the world is this man?"

"A true revolutionary, I think. Some actually call him the Messiah."

"Is he from the House of David?"

The young man bit his lower lip. "They say he often makes that claim. He is very precise about that."

"I see. But to make women his equal." The old scribe nodded his head disapprovingly. "Honor them, yes. But to relinquish absolute authority—I don't know. It's . . . it's disturbing."

"Perhaps . . . perhaps there's something there to be considered."

The old scribe took his hand off the young man's shoulder as he shrugged his own. "I don't know what to make of this younger generation sometimes. I suppose if a man is willing to suffer the consequences of an independent woman under his own roof, then let him."

"I believe all he's saying is there's a true gain in treating a woman as a person."

"A person, fine. But equal—rough, very rough. I believe if you and those of your generation continue with these notions—"

"Not my notions—"

"I know, I know—nevertheless: you'll probably live to regret it, my son. You do realize, of course, there's even some question concerning their possession of a soul. But that's the least of this man's controversy. What worries me are his obvious associates."

"You mean, Judas."

"Specifically, yes. And he approached you?"

"Yes."

"Hmm. Our youngest—and most vulnerable."

"Not so vulnerable."

"Yes, yes, I know." The old man placed a comforting hand on the young scribe's shoulder. "And what made that man think the Sanhedrin needed his cooperation to have this so-called prophet, Jesus, arrested?"

"They just thought—"

"They?"

"He. He thought in matters concerning the Law—"

"We need no help from the likes of a gentile," the old scribe said firmly.

"Then you do know who he is?" He caught a glint in the old man's eyes. "Yes. Of course you do. But remember, he's a professed Jew."

"A convert, yes, I know."

"And he has every right to accuse those who are breaking the Law."

"But what Law has this learned rabbi broken that he couldn't fully justify?" The old scribe shook his head. "No. We have no real quarrel with this man, Jesus. The Pharisees and the Sadducees in general—including the Supreme Council—are also not enemies of this so-called prophet among many who, between you and me, might even assist Israel toward true liberation."

"On the contrary, he's a hindrance. He often dilutes the anger of insurgency with mixed signals."

"Then it won't be to our interest to protect him from Rome."

"Or from Herod."

The old man lifted his hand from the young scribe's shoulder and invited him to walk alongside him. "And as for Judas, well, he's relatively new in his understanding of the Law."

"But surely it doesn't take a genius to know when a man like Jesus has overstepped his bounds."

"We've heard others who've claimed he might be the Messiah. All Judas has done is support this claim. Isn't that so?"

"Well—actually, Judas has claimed more than that," the young man said nervously. "He's claimed Jesus to be the son . . . " He moved closer to the old scribe so he wouldn't be overheard. " . . . to be the son of God."

The old scribe stopped walking and turned toward the young scribe with a dumbfounded expression on his face. "You . . . you heard this with your own ears?"

"Yes. He confessed this to Judas and his following, then swore them to secrecy."

"He confessed to being a god—"

"The son of—"

"Yes, yes—then demanded an oath of secrecy."

"That's right."

The old scribe began to laugh gently. "Then Jesus is a clown." His laughter continued until he was almost unable to contain himself. "Do you expect the High Court of Seventy to be concerned over a crazy man? Nobody. Nobody in their right mind would listen to him in earnest."

"Yes, yes, at first those were my thoughts exactly. But then . . . then I began to wonder: what if his disciples *are* listening?"

"Not to that. That's why the sworn secrecy to his select few. See?"

"True, true."

"He's a passing fancy. A fad. You'll see. He's of no political consequence."

"True, true, all true. But—"

"What?"

"There's one thing more."

"Alright then, out with it."

The young scribe bit his lip again. "Well—Judas offered me a purse."

"Oh? And?"

"It was a purse full of silver—an offering to the high court."

The old scribe's face turned grave. "I hope . . . I hope that wasn't intended as some kind of a bribe."

"Well—it was."

"Go on."

The young man broke out into a cold sweat. "He just thought since he had this information available—"

"Concerning Jesus' claim to be, ugh, you know—"

"Yes—that I could deliver this silver to the court in the hope that this madman Jesus could be ignored."

"How much?"

"I believe it was thirty weights of silver."

"How much?" The old man grabbed the front of his own tunic as if he were suffering chest pains and allowed his cane to fall to the ground. "First of all, did he really think he could buy men of God with thirty pieces of silver? For any reason? And secondly, this absurd and blasphemous claim, this . . . this, you ought to know better!"

"I was only passing on this information." The young man retrieved the cane and handed it to the old man.

"I'm sorry, I know. I'm sorry." The old scribe leaned against his cane. "Now, listen. We're going to do that man Judas, and ourselves, a favor. We're going to pretend he never approached you. He doesn't exist." He started walking and invited the young man to come along. "And I advise you not to approach anybody else concerning this matter. Say no more about this," he said, unable to mask his agitation and concern. "Because if this kind of information were to succeed in reaching the High Court with your name, somehow, still associated with this man's claim, well, it's not out of the realm that your life could be endangered."

"But as you've admitted yourself: this man would be considered a clown."

"Yes. Him, perhaps. But not you or this Judas. But especially you—almost a lawyer for heaven sake. It's possible you'd live just long enough to be placed against a wall to be stoned. What a terrible way to end a promising career."

"Are we living in a time so completely devoid of tolerance?"

"It's not a pretty death. You know that."

The young man nervously licked his lips. "I do."

"Good. Let's not talk anymore of this. Come on, to the inner courts. There's someone I want to introduce you to."

The old man took the young man by the arm and escorted him toward a set of stairs leading up into the inner courts.

CHAPTER 13

The Fourth Watch: Facing Eternity

The darkness smothered him like a blind man's nightmare. He was suffocating—suffocating!

Judas stumbled, then fell headlong near the mouth of an alleyway. The impact of his chest slamming against the hard muddy ground forced out the last reserve of his breath and distorted his perception concerning the passage of time. He opened his eyes first, then involuntarily gasped for air: a respiratory pursuit manifested by a hollow groan. His second groan provoked a threatening growl from a nearby dog, accompanied by the skittish bark of another. He turned his head as he pushed his torso off the ground by extending his arms and locking his elbows into a four-point support: on the palms of his hands and on the caps of his knees.

He smelled the mound of stinking garbage before he finally saw the occupying force of scavenging dogs—one of them snapped at him while another began to bark more aggressively.

"Mangy dogs!"

Judas sat back on his knees, picked up a stone, and threw it at one of the silhouettes. The stone missed its mark, but it caused the pack to scatter and scurry about their precious territory—each dog increasing the frequency and intensity of their barking. He picked up another stone as he stood up with the aid of the nearby wall and threw it. The yelp that followed gave him a moment of cruel satisfaction.

"Take that you mongrel bitch!"

But the satisfaction was short-lived and the misery that was tormenting him pushed him northward toward the Damascus Gate in order to escape Jerusalem once and for all.

The gatekeeper stood near the needle's eye under a hanging lantern that provided the immediate vicinity with a weak and restricted light. Feeble as the lamp was, it still caused Judas to squint and cower from its luminosity.

"What? You again?" the gatekeeper said.

"I'll not be through here again, I promise you."

"From what I can see of your appearance, you best not be."

"I've done nothing to be arrested."

The gatekeeper ignored him. He lifted the thick cross beam off the pair of hooks that held it in place and opened the small wooden door, which was built into the massive gate. "Pass. Quickly."

"I've broken no law."

"Whatever. I don't care." The gatekeeper looked over his shoulder. "But if I were you, I'd care. These damn

Syrian legionnaires will be marching past here soon." Then he looked up at his hanging lamp. "I hope they can spare me a little oil for my lamp. I didn't have time—"

"Have you a spare lamp—or a torch?"

"No. No torch." The gatekeeper leaned the crossbeam against the gate and unhooked his oil lamp enclosed in a hanging lantern. "Oil. Strictly oil caged in my lantern."

"Don't worry, I'm not going to steal your lamp."

"Then pass, go on, pass." The gatekeeper looked through the opened door as Judas hesitated. "Such ominous weather. Where has it come from? I was even late in closing the gate this evening." Suddenly remembering Judas's presence. "Pass already, will you. Go on. You act as if there's something bad waiting for you on the other side."

"Nothing. Nothing awaits me."

"You'll get no sympathy from anyone with talk like that."

Judas walked through the needle's eye and felt the blackness close in on him again. Then he froze in place when he heard the gatekeeper shut the door and replace the crossbeam. The air felt different and the dark road endless.

For one brief moment, he thought about going to Golgotha. But what would have been the point? Done. All deeds had been done, intentional or not—all was irreversible and, therefore, over.

He started walking. There was no need to hurry. There was nobody pursuing him but himself. He no longer mattered to anybody. He'd been used and misused, then discarded by all the factions involved. He proceeded toward his destination feeling neutral, looking nowhere, seeking nothing, anticipating death.

He approached the door of Dinah's tavern. The place was already closed and the cracks between the window shutters were not glowing with interior light.

"I'll show that bitch a thing or two."

He raised his fist to bang on the door, but it remained suspended in the air.

"No. I'll not waste what's left of my contempt."

He lowered his arm and backed away from the door as he removed his leather belt and tied it around his neck. Then he walked out from under the crudely built portico and looked up at the sky.

"Lord. Lord. Take back your gift called life. I can't bear its burden any longer. You . . . you've . . ." He dropped onto his knees and wept bitterly.

When he was through, he stood up, drained of what was left of any meaning which might have provided a motive for his continued existence.

He noticed a large empty clay pot, rolled it underneath the portico's main rafter, set the pot base up, and climbed on top. Then he lashed the end of the belt around the rafter, gave it a tug to test its strength, and unceremoniously tilted the pot away from his feet without the slightest hesitation.

The agony of strangulation was such a physical shock that his appendages convulsed and the fingers of his hands involuntarily tore at the belt around his throat. But as soon as he realized that his right hand was reaching for the standing end of the belt, his iron-willed madness made that arm go limp even though his other limbs continued to thrash and tremble uncontrollably.

No longer able to blink, his bulging eyes watched life's final assault as his body continued to fight. But he won, despite his body's desperate battle for the continuance of existence; he won, as he lost what was left of his life.

CHAPTER 14
After Sunrise

Lila remained at the open doorway's threshold of the tavern as Dinah approached Judas's lifeless body hanging from the main rafter of her modest portico.

"Lord, Lord," Dinah sighed. "How are we going to explain this?"

"It's a good thing neither of us went to bed with him. He was mad."

Dinah's expression was full of bewilderment as she edged closer to Judas. "Don't worry, Lila. I don't think insanity can be caught by having sex."

"You don't think so?"

"No. And I don't really think he was mad."

"Then what do you think was wrong with him?"

"Oh, it was nothing. Nothing but religion. Nothing that has any answer for it."

"Meaning—politics?"

"That's what I just said," Dinah snapped irritably.

Lila became self-conscious. "There's much I don't understand."

"And you're in good company. I'm sorry." Dinah studied Judas's pitiful body:

There were thick strands of hair crisscrossing his bruised face, made more grotesque by the thick blue tongue protruding from the gape of his mouth. His billowing tunic was torn and blood-stained and encrusted with muck and refuse; his feet and sandals were almost encased in mud, and the lower half of his full length tunic was drenched with wet sewage. He smelled of excrement so foul that even the carrion birds would have found it difficult to make a meal of him.

Dinah covered her mouth and nose with a corner of her upper mantle that she had carelessly draped over her shoulders. Then she took a couple of steps backward to assess the overall scene:

"He must have used his own belt as a noose around his neck. Yes. He must have rolled that wide pot—large enough to stand on—underneath that sturdy rafter, turned the pot over so the base of it was up, climbed on top, lashed the other end of his belt around the rafter, and then . . . then kicked the pot away." Dinah shook her head, then glanced back at Lila. "There it is: no separation—the results of politics and religion—"

"And silver, I think."

"You're a quick study, Lila. You should give yourself more credit."

"I'm nothing."

"Yes, well—we're all nothing." Dinah indicated Judas with a single nod, "Nothing but remains."

"Everything remains."

"Yes. Even his religion, whatever that was—the poor tormented idiot."

"What should we do?"

"Do? Nothing. Just leave him. One of Ganto's men will see or hear of this soon enough. They'll take care of it for us—I hope. Besides, it's their doing."

"But Rome and—"

"It's all their doing! *Men*." Dinah inhaled deeply to control her anger, then exhaled slowly to release some of her bitterness. "Damn ... their ... deeds." Lila remained silent and apprehensive as Dinah turned away from Judas and started walking toward her. "But most of all, damn them for what they've done to my Azriel. Damn the whole human race."

As Lila stepped aside to allow Dinah to pass, she stole a final glance at Judas, then shut the door as she followed her mistress inside.

The Thieves of Golgotha

Lliteras' novel is a thought-provoking retelling of the crucifixion from the viewpoint of Nikos and Azriel, the two thieves who died alongside Jesus. Taking a well-known biblical story and expanding on it is always a risky proposition, but Lliteras provides fully rounded characterizations, not only of the thieves, but of Bartholomew, Barrabbas, and Jesus himself. Recommended.

—*Library Journal*

Long condemned to the margins of crucifixion scenes, *The Thieves of Golgotha* comes to life in a sympathetic fictional portrait from D.S. Lliteras, who traces their lives of crime from slavery to freedom to death on the cross.

—*Publishers Weekly*

Regardless of your religious orientation, you will be deeply moved by the latest novel by D.S. Lliteras—*The Thieves of Golgotha*. If you read two pages you will not be able to put this book down, and you will never be the same after reading it. This is the book you will buy and then get a copy for everyone you value. Promise.

—*Lynx, A Journal for Linking Poets*

Virginia Beach author emerges as a promising voice in contemporary literature.

—*Port Folio Weekly*

The Thieves of Golgotha

There is an authentic sweat-producing sense of being under sentence in *Thieves*, an awful awareness of the fragility of life and the terrifying prospect of pain. Lliteras spares no detail of the culminating brutality, featuring instruments like the flagrum, 'dressed with lead weights and sharp bone and pointed scorpions at the ends of the multiple-thronged whip.' His graphic explanation of the crucifixion is harrowing.

—*The Virginian-Pilot*

Lliteras's unflinching flesh-and-blood examination of the condemned men's ordeal will inspire a new understanding of the meaning of the crucifixion.

—*barnesandnoble.com—Fiction and Literature*

Danny Lliteras is an intelligent guy. And he's really a writer. If you're interested in unusual fiction, check out his new novel.

—*The Portsmouth Currents*

The Thieves of Golgotha is a powerfully written biblical tale, told mainly through dialogue, of the two thieves who were crucified with Jesus.

—*The VVA Veteran*

The Thieves of Golgotha

The New Testament makes brief mention of the two thieves who flanked Christ in the hill of the skull. D.S. Lliteras draws these men out of the biblical background and places them center stage in *The Thieves of Golgotha*. Beginning with their confinement in the blackness of a Roman prison, the novel hauls you into the horror of impending execution, lurching from one torment to the next until you find yourself wishing that these two reprehensible men could find even a momentary reprieve—a level of identification between reader and antihero forged in rare talent. Lliteras's brutal descriptions paint scenes with a harsh reality that drags you deeper into the novel even as you instinctively try to avert your eyes. In contemporary dialogue strongly reminiscent of that in Hemingway's fiction, Lliteras's characters tell their personal stories of incarceration, doubt, pain, and salvation on a human level, where spiritual discovery is grasped with the gut, not with the brain.

—*Amazon.com—Brian Patterson*

The Thieves of Golgotha isn't your usual novel about Jesus' crucifixion: it's told from the viewpoint of the two felons crucified alongside him, and creates an absorbing counterplot of intrigue and detail to add life and adventure to what at first glance seems the usual story line.

—*The Midwest Book Review—The Bookwatch*

In the Heart of Things

The narrative is dotted with spontaneous poems and small illumina-tions...like moments in literature created by the poets of consciousness (Joyce, Salinger, Kerouac, in my book...). I've always wondered what the novel to follow Maugham's *The Razor's Edge* would be like.... Lliteras has written just such a novel.

—*Inner Journeys—Literary Review*

Into the Ashes

D.S. Lliteras has penned a compelling tale of friendship, caring, and the discovery of what is really important in life. Interwoven with his poi-gnant and inspired poetry, this is destined to become a literary classic.

—*The Paperback Trader*

Half-Hidden by Twilight

Author Daniel S. Lliteras is a compelling writer able to portray the harsh realities of life.... His literary grasp virtually wrings the innermost thoughts of his characters for exposure on the pages of his books, mak-ing the reader vulnerable to the pangs of hunger, dreariness, life, death, wisdom, love, happiness and loss, shedding light on all of the complexi-ties of heart and mind.

—*Naples Daily News—The Books Page*

In a Warrior's Romance

Romance is nothing more than 200 pages of Minolta snapshots and brief snatches of haiku verse. But, for those acquainted with military conflict, it packs the punch of *War and Peace*.

—*The Virginian-Pilot*

D.S. Lliteras is the author of five
previously published books.
He currently resides in Virginia Beach,
Virginia with his wife, Kathleen.

Hampton Roads Publishing Company
publishes and distributes books on a variety of subjects,
including metaphysics, health, complementary medicine,
visionary fiction, and other related topics.

To order books or to receive a copy of our latest catalog,
call toll-free, (800) 766-8009,
or send your name and address to:

Hampton Roads Publishing Company, Inc.
134 Burgess Lane
Charlottesville, VA 22902
e-mail: hrpc@hrpub.com
www.hrpub.com